"It's strange. Being here again."

Stephanie scanned the room. "Brings back memories."

"Any good ones?" The question slipped out.

She lowered her chin. "A few."

"Well, most of my memories of us together were good." Tom kept his voice low. The past pressed against his chest, his heart craving the release of honesty. All the times he'd blamed her for ruining his life had overshadowed one big fact: he'd loved her, loved being married to her, and those days, for him, had been good.

"Most of them?" She picked at the edge of her sweater.

"Until we fell apart."

"Are you sure your memory isn't tricking you?" Her tone held no trace of sarcasm.

"It's not. I might not have been what you needed, but that time was special for me." He grazed her hand.

She glanced at him, questions in her eyes.

"I know we can't go back," he said. "I just wanted you to know. I was happy being married to you."

Jill Kemerer writes novels with love, humor and faith. Besides spoiling her mini dachshund and keeping up with her busy kids, Jill reads stacks of books, lives for her morning coffee and gushes over fluffy animals. She resides in Ohio with her husband and two children. Jill loves connecting with readers, so please visit her website, jillkemerer.com, or contact her at PO Box 2802, Whitehouse, OH 43571.

Books by Jill Kemerer

Love Inspired

Small-Town Bachelor
Unexpected Family

Unexpected Family

Jill Kemerer

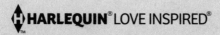

HARLEQUIN® LOVE INSPIRED®

Recycling programs
for this product may
not exist in your area.

LOVE INSPIRED BOOKS

ISBN-13: 978-0-373-81863-1

Unexpected Family

www.Harlequin.com

Printed in U.S.A.

How long must I wrestle with my thoughts
and day after day have sorrow in my heart?
—*Psalms* 13:2

For Olivia and Brandon.
You make me a better person.
I'm blessed by you each day!

Chapter One

Stephanie Sheffield climbed the creaking steps of the tan bungalow nestled in a clearing of dense woods. The covered porch looked lonely. A welcome mat would go a long way to cheer the space. If she owned a home like this, she would bring it to life with bundles of corn husks, pumpkins and a pot or two of burgundy mums.

But she wasn't here to mentally redecorate.

Guilt had consumed her for five years. A sixth year wasn't an option. Stomach tightening, Stephanie knocked.

Seconds ticked by without any movement inside. Maybe he wasn't home. Maybe she had the wrong address. Or maybe God was giving her a grace period.

Grace? God may have forgiven her, but she still had to pay for her sins.

Stephanie rapped louder and turned to view the

property. She half expected a deer to leap onto the lawn, moist from an autumn drizzle. Crimson leaves fluttered down from a tall maple, and the cobalt blue of Michigan's Lake Endwell peeked through in the distance. The lake threatened to unleash memories, ones she couldn't afford to think about right now.

A lone figure jogged down the country road. He rounded the drive, and her muscles tensed.

Tom.

Did he still hate her?

If he didn't, he soon would.

Drawing closer, he slowed to a walk. Shock flashed in those sink-into-them blue eyes, eyes that once lured her. Tousled dark brown hair softened his cheekbones. His straight nose pointed to a determined chin. He looked more athletic, more rugged than she remembered. Why couldn't he have aged badly? And why did seeing him again make her feel as though she'd downed a warm cup of tea?

Stephanie leaned against the peeling porch rail and winced as pain shot up her rib cage. Now that he'd appeared, she had no idea what to say. Everything she'd rehearsed during the thirty-minute drive jumbled in her brain.

"What happened?" Tom closed the distance between them, reaching to touch her bruised cheek, but he snatched his hand back before making contact. His unexpected tenderness almost undid her. She chased away the sudden yearning for his touch.

"It's nothing. I was in an accident yesterday. My car was totaled, but I'm fine. Bruised ribs. A few scratches."

"Why are you here?" The tenderness was snuffed out like the candles she lit to chase away smells in her apartment.

"Is there somewhere we can talk?" She shifted her weight from one foot to the other. "Inside maybe?"

"Why?" He crossed his arms over his broad chest.

Because I'm about to shatter your world, and even strong Tom Sheffield will need a seat for this.

She gestured to the door.

He stood taller, legs shoulder width apart, intimidating in his gray sweatshirt and black shorts. The old Stephanie would have let him call the shots. But the old Stephanie had been a girl, not a woman in control of her life.

"It's important." A breeze played with the hair around her neck. She brushed it aside.

Finally he nodded, opening the faded red door. The living room, while tidy, lacked color. The only pictures were of some stadium and what appeared to be an autographed photo of a baseball team. A dark leather couch, love seat, matching chair and a huge television filled the room. No cozy aromas like vanilla or cinnamon lurked in the air.

She sat on the couch as he lowered his body into the chair. She'd mentally rehearsed this moment a million times. Gotten in her car to confess at least twice a week. Picked up the phone to tell him, to explain. And now she was here and her vocal chords went on strike.

"So?" He opened his hands, giving her a pointed look. Stephanie couldn't tell if his gruff manner was real or an act, but it didn't matter.

"There's no easy way to say this," she said. "I've wanted to. I've tried. But the accident yesterday—well, it got me here when nothing else would." The rest of her speech stuck in her throat. His clenched jaw didn't ease her nerves.

"Well, could you move things along?" He tapped his fingers against his thigh. "I've got another hour of training to get in."

"Training?" The Tom she'd known had been driven by work. By success. He'd rarely spent time exercising or, for that matter, on anything outside his car dealership. He'd preferred his job to her.

"Look, I don't have time for chitchat. If you have something to say, say it." He shot to his feet, but he seemed more uncomfortable than angry.

"There's no good way to do this, so I'm going to be blunt." *Say it. Do it. Get it over with.* "You have a daughter."

His mouth dropped open. He shut it. Opened it again.

Stephanie's legs instinctively prepared to run, but she didn't move. The expressions crumpling his face hit her harder than tears ever could. The man's world had just imploded, and she'd launched the bomb. What could she possibly say? Sorry?

Sorry wasn't good enough, and neither was she.

His chest expanded. Cheekbones strained against skin, and the vulnerability, the pain she'd witnessed, vanished, replaced by something cold, something that would have broken her before she became a believer. She girded herself.

"What kind of joke is this?" His tone was lethal, the words quiet.

"It's not a joke."

Tom stared at her as if she'd grown two horns and a tail. Maybe she had.

"A daughter?" He shook his head. "No."

"Yes."

His face drained of its healthy glow, replaced by a tinge of avocado green. "What's her name?"

She hesitated, not expecting the question. What had she expected? Him to order her to get out?

Absolutely. A slew of angry accusations? Yes. But the name? "Macy."

"Macy," he murmured. His glare was penetrating before confusion clouded it. "How? When?"

"She's four. She'll be five on April 20."

He paced, growing six inches taller, everything about him bigger, restless. "Why didn't you tell me?"

She'd tried to justify not telling him—oh, how she'd tried—but only one of her reasons held up. Why would he care she'd stupidly thought she'd hurt him enough? That she'd feared he'd want to stay together for the baby's sake? That she couldn't, wouldn't put him through a lifetime of being married to her?

"Remember the last thing you said to me?" Stephanie said softly. A flash of recognition crossed his face. She rose, setting her hand on the back of the couch to steady herself. "You said, 'At least we didn't have kids.'"

"I said a lot of stupid things that night. You should have told me you were pregnant."

"I didn't know I was pregnant then, and you served me with divorce papers the next week." Stephanie trailed her finger over the leather. "But you're right. I should have told you as soon as I found out. I was scared. Ashamed. I'd messed up our marriage. And I didn't want to trap you into staying with me."

If she could go back, be the person she was now instead of the insecure girl who married him… But she couldn't. And it didn't excuse him, either. His constant hours away had made it clear his job was number one. Macy deserved better than to be ignored.

"Not good enough." The clipped words proved how much this was costing him. "Not when we're talking about another life."

"I know." She tamped down the words battling to come out. His pale eyes held her captive, dared her to tell him the truth. What was the truth? "I told myself you'd moved on, so why disrupt your life? For all I knew, you could have gotten remarried, started your own family. You'd resent me barging into your world. But I know I was selfish." Standing in front of him now, she could see how selfish she was.

"You're telling me I have a daughter. *A daughter.*" He thrust his hand through his dark hair, his face haunted. "And I'm supposed to take your word about all this?"

Now *that* question she'd been expecting. She fumbled for her purse. "I have a picture."

"Why are you doing this? Why now?"

"Because you deserve to know. You've always deserved to know, and Macy does, too. I can't live with the guilt anymore. I'm sorry." She swiped her phone and opened the photos to Macy's smiling face. *God, whatever happens here, don't let it hurt my precious girl.* She held it out to him. "Here. See for yourself."

He didn't accept it, but the pulse in his cheek throbbed—he clearly wrestled emotions. It wasn't as if she'd fooled herself into thinking this meeting would be easy, but the reality of it? Brutal.

"Just look at the picture," she said. "Take it."

He took it from her hand. He blinked twice, his face relaxing. Then he snapped his attention to her. "She…"

Please let him see the obvious.

"My eyes…" He held it closer, peering at it. "She's beautiful."

"She is. She has your eyebrows, too. And your lips. She's all yours."

"Macy." He traced his finger around the screen. He glanced up, recognition pushing the stress off his face. "Mine. I have a daughter."

Out of all the scenarios she'd considered, she'd never allowed herself to hope he'd be happy. The full weight of what she'd done, what she had kept from him—how much she'd taken from him— slammed into her. Another thing she'd feel guilty about the rest of her life.

Tom handed her the phone, then wiped his hand over his face. "I don't know where to start."

"Ask me anything." She propped her hands on the back of the couch for support.

"Do you still live in Petoskey?"

"No. I moved to Kalamazoo last year to finish college." With a semester and a half left of her undergraduate program in accounting, Stephanie could practically taste success. In less than three years, she'd be a successful CPA. A role model. Someone Macy could be proud of. All the struggles she'd been through would be worth it to give Macy a better life.

"So you're telling me you've lived half an hour away and it just occurred to you now to tell me I have a daughter?" He pushed his sleeves up.

"It's occurred to me every day since I saw two lines on the pregnancy test." Her ribs ached, but she didn't dare sit again.

"I can't believe this." His voice broke, and his strained face tore her up inside.

"I'm sorry. I'm so sorry."

"I'm sorry, too. I'm sorry *our child* has lived without a father her whole life. Or…wait. Let me guess. She hasn't lived without a father, has she?"

Stephanie couldn't breathe. Couldn't move. The accusation cut, but he had every right to say that to her. Every right. The clock on the wall ticked as she tried to figure out a reply.

"There hasn't been a man in my life since our divorce. Until last year Macy and I lived with Dad, but he moved to Miami when I went back to school." Her energy dissolved, and she fought to stay upright.

"I want to see her." He stood, wide-legged, a fist on each hip.

"Okay, we can figure—"

"I want to see her now."

"But she—"

"I want to see my daughter today."

Stephanie's mind swirled. "She's in day care for another hour, but, Tom, she doesn't know any of this."

"Well, that makes two of us. It's about time she does."

"I agree she needs to know. It's one of the reasons I'm here today. She's been all over me about daddies and sisters and brothers. I told her she would meet her father when the time was right, and she accepted it. But she's young. Producing a dad out of the blue… Well, I don't want to traumatize her."

"Kind of like when I saw you holding hands with another guy when you told me you were shopping with Tiffany?"

"I crossed a line, but I never cheated on you, Tom." Her throat burned. Of course he'd throw that in her face. "I don't want to introduce you to her as her father unless you plan on being a *permanent* part of her life. She's not someone you can blow off for work. And you wonder why I didn't tell you. You hate me."

"I don't." His posture relaxed a fraction.

Did regret shine in his eyes? She doubted it. Telling him about Macy had thrown them right where they'd left off—unable to be together in the same room. Did she dare add their daughter to this unstable mix?

"I just want to see my child." His tone sounded reasonable.

"I understand. But I'm not freaking her out by springing a dad on her today. The accident yesterday was bad enough."

"Was she hurt? Is she okay?"

"She has a sprained wrist. Nothing a sling and time won't heal." She sighed. She'd gone over all the possibilities, knew there was a chance he'd demand to see Macy right away. Knew, too, he might refuse to allow Macy in his life. What if he met her and decided being a dad wasn't for him? Stephanie fought back a groan. She owed him the right to make the decision. "Why don't you meet us at McDonald's in an hour and a half? We can say you're an old friend of mine."

"I'm not lying to her."

She pinched the bridge of her nose. "I don't

want to lie to her, either, but do we have to tell her tonight?"

"Fine." His shoulders dropped. "We'll do it your way. For now."

From the front seat of his truck, Tom glimpsed the golden arches. A hundred years had passed since Stephanie left an hour and a half ago. Seeing her on his porch had brought back all of it—the day they'd met, how quickly he'd fallen in love with her, their short engagement, their shorter marriage.

He hadn't been enough for her.

Only Stephanie could manage to throw his life off course when he'd finally found a way to get it back on track.

This morning he'd been checking invoices, calling his assistant managers and planning his training session for the day. Forty-two weeks left plenty of time to build strength and endurance for his first IRONMAN competition. And nothing would stop him from finishing in less than twelve hours. The average competitor finished in twelve and a half.

He was done being average.

Signing up for the triathlon had given his life meaning again. Something to strive for. Something to feel proud of.

But this...a child...changed everything.

He closed his eyes. Emotions drained him empty like at the end of a tough workout. And now he had to walk in there and meet his daughter without letting her know who he was. He'd almost called his sister Claire earlier. She knew how to handle these situations. She'd be able to tell him if Stephanie was being reasonable or manipulative. But if he called Claire, he'd have to explain…and he was not ready to tell anyone in his large family he was a father. He might not ever be ready.

God, help me out here? I don't know what to say. I've barely been around kids, and now I'm meeting mine for the first time. What if I mess up? What if I scare her? Maybe Stephanie was right not to tell Macy I'm her dad yet.

Another minute ticked by before he got the nerve to hop out of his truck. Shoving his keys into the pocket of his jeans, he straightened his long-sleeved black T-shirt. He could do this, meet Macy without intimidating her.

Inside, he scanned the busy restaurant to find Stephanie. Typical fast-food sounds surrounded him—the beeps of the registers, the muted chatter of customers waiting in line and the occasional shout of a kid. The place smelled like French fries. His heartbeat paused at the sight of Stephanie sitting next to the little girl with dark brown waves flowing down her back. The child didn't look up until he stopped at their table.

"Thanks for joining us." Stephanie's tone was pleasant, assertive, but she couldn't mask the uncertainty in her eyes. "Macy, this is an old friend of mine, Tom."

The girl's tiny face with creamy skin and raspberry lips stole his breath. Even prettier than her picture. Her faded-blue-jean eyes matched his exactly. It took everything in him not to swoop her up and crush her to him. He knew in an instant he would do anything—anything—for this little girl.

"Hi, Macy. How's your arm?" He gestured to the black sling and sat across from her at the table. His knee bounced triple time.

"It doesn't hurt. I don't need this anymore." She started ripping the Velcro from her sling, but Stephanie placed her hand over it.

"The doctor said you have to wear it for a few weeks."

Macy pushed her bottom lip out. "It's 'noying, Mama."

"I know. But it's there for your wrist to heal."

She grimaced, dunking a chicken nugget into barbecue sauce before taking a nibble. Stephanie's gaze darted here and there like a wild rabbit's, and the silence stretched to uncomfortable proportions.

What now? He had no idea what to say to either of them. Didn't have much experience with kids. Or ex-wives. If he had known—

He could have what? *Prepared? Yeah, right.*

"Did you want something to eat?" Stephanie's smile was tight around the edges.

The bruises couldn't hide her delicate bone structure, the rich brown of her eyes. Her hair was a little shorter than he remembered, but just as dark and shiny. He'd been so caught up in the revelation of having a daughter, he'd barely registered Stephanie until this moment.

"Uh." He hadn't eaten since lunch, but he wasn't hungry, either. "I'm not sure."

Macy cupped her hand around her mouth as she whispered loudly to Stephanie. "Why is he here if he's not eating?" Stephanie gave him a pointed look.

What an idiot. Here he was, a strange guy showing up at their meal and not ordering anything. Even a kid knew it was fishy. No wonder Stephanie worried.

"Maybe I'll get a salad." He rapped his knuckles on the table.

"Are you sure about that, mister?" Macy frowned. "Salad has lettuce and tomatoes in it. My grandpa always gets a cheeseburger when he comes here."

He grinned. "I like cheeseburgers and fries, too, but I have to eat healthy."

"Why?"

"I'm training for a triathlon."

She munched on a fry. "What's a…tri…what'd you call it?"

"A triathlon. It's called the IRONMAN competition."

"Noah has an Iron Man backpack. Do you get a red suit, too?" Her hopeful expression made him want to tell her yes, he'd be the real Iron Man when he crossed the finish line. But he shook his head.

"No, it's not that kind of Iron Man. It's where a bunch of people swim, ride their bikes and run. It's a race."

"I have to use training wheels. Tatum has pink sparkly streamers on her bike, but mine doesn't have any." The pitiful look she gave her mother almost made Tom chuckle. *Cute.* He could get used to her matter-of-fact tone and still-developing pronunciation. No, he *would* get used to it.

"You're blessed to have a bike at all, Macy." Stephanie pointed to the Happy Meal. "Keep eating those nuggets."

"Yes, Mama."

"Do you like swimming, Macy? I live right next to a big lake. My brothers and dad and I go fishing all summer."

Stephanie's wary glance speared him, but he kept his attention on Macy.

"My grandpa and I make sand castles at the beach. But Mommy and I moved to a 'partment." She sipped her chocolate milk. "I'm going to tell Noah about the race. He takes swim lessons, but he's too scared to jump off the board. Do you think if he jumps in the pool, he could be the Iron Man, too?"

Tom nodded. "Sure. When he gets older. Anyone who finishes the race is an Iron Man."

"You silly pants, there's only one." She wiggled her finger, and her face lit up.

Stephanie ran her hand over Macy's hair. "The IRONMAN Tom's talking about isn't what you're thinking."

Best to let Stephanie explain. He went to the register, waited for the salad, then slid back into his seat.

"I'm going to kin-dee-garden when I'm five." She held out five splayed fingers with her free hand.

"Wow, kindergarten."

Macy continued, "I can count real high."

"How high?" He tore the packet of dressing open and watched her out of the corner of his eye.

"Real high. One, two, three…"

When she got to forty-five, Stephanie touched her arm. "Okay, we got it. You're a good counter."

"I can go higher," she said.

"Honey, I have no doubt you could count to a

million if you put your mind to it, but we need to finish up dinner and head back home. I have a paper to complete." Stephanie raised the jacket from the back of her chair and draped it over Macy's shoulders.

Tom covered his half-eaten salad. What now? Did Stephanie plan on leaving without giving him her contact information? She didn't think she could just show up, tell him about their daughter and expect life to continue as if nothing happened, did she? This was his child, and whether she liked it or not, he wasn't disappearing, nor was he going to pretend he was an old friend for long.

"Before I forget, here." Stephanie slipped him a piece of paper. "My cell number and home phone. After seven is best. I work and go to school. It gets crazy around dinnertime." She wrangled Macy's arm into the jacket but couldn't quite cover the sling. Then she smiled. "Thanks, Tom, for…everything."

"I'll be in touch." He stood, holding his hand out to Macy. "Nice to meet you."

She took his hand. "Nice to meet you, too."

"Till next time." And he left. In the cool air, his exhilaration and nerves about the meeting seeped out like a leaky tire.

He'd missed more than four years of her life.

He unlocked his truck, got in, raised his gaze to the ceiling and rubbed his jaw.

Macy. Macy Sheffield. He closed his eyes, recalling her sweet face. If only he had a picture of her. What had she looked like as a baby? How had she been? Fussy? No, of course not. Not his darling.

He started the truck, his thoughts racing as the engine rumbled to life. He'd missed her first tooth. First steps. First words.

Were there any firsts left? Had he missed them all?

Checking his mirrors, he backed out of the spot. He wasn't missing any more of her life. But what would Macy need him for? Nothing came to mind.

What about tne streamers? The pink sparkly streamers. Yeah. And piggyback rides. And ice cream. Every kid liked ice cream. He'd let her pretend to drive the cars in the showroom. Owning two auto dealerships had its perks. Take her to baseball games and buy her Barbies and protect her from boys.

He'd be the best dad ever.

And someday he might be able to forgive Stephanie for keeping her from him.

Chapter Two

Stephanie made it home without the expected questions about Tom, mainly by distracting Macy with a Disney CD. Nothing like princesses singing movie tunes to buy a little quiet time. As first meetings went, Stephanie would give tonight five stars. No awkward questions, no heated words, just a man and a little girl getting to know each other. She'd made the right decision to tell Tom about Macy.

After giving Macy a quick bath and getting her into her turtle pajamas, Stephanie sat next to her on the couch and drew a soft purple throw over them both.

"How's my kitten?" She pulled Macy into her arms.

"I'm not a kitty." Macy giggled, snuggling closer.

"You're not? But you're cute as a kitten. And you purr, right?"

"Prrr…" Macy pretended to lick the back of her hand.

Stephanie's mind wandered. Seeing Tom brought it all back—how much she'd admired him when she was a twenty-year-old college student. How amazed she'd been that gorgeous, could-have-any-girl Tom Sheffield even noticed her. Twenty-five and with a business degree had made him more alluring. He'd made her feel special, pretty, like someone better than ordinary old her. Six months later when they got married, he promptly quit his dead-end job to join the family business. She soon learned work always came first.

"Is Tom your boyfriend?" Macy curled their fingers together.

The questions had begun. Stephanie stroked Macy's hair and inhaled the scent of fruity shampoo, so innocent and sweet. "No, no, nothing like that. We were friends a long time ago. He heard we were in an accident and wanted to make sure we were okay."

"Oh. Why didn't Grandpa come?"

"Grandpa didn't know. Remember, he's in Florida now."

"I miss him. Let's go see him."

"That's the plan, toots. Less than a year and we'll be living with Grandpa again. We can go to the beach every day. No snow. No cold. Just sunshine."

"Yay! I can't wait to live with Grandpa again."

"I know. I can't, either." As soon as she finished her degree, she and Macy were moving back in with her dad. They'd lived with him in Petoskey until last year when he retired and bought a condo in Miami. She and Macy almost joined him, but Western University offered her a full scholarship only available to single mothers, and the University of Miami wouldn't give her any financial aid.

Dad had offered to pay, but he couldn't afford expensive tuition on his fixed income. Besides, Stephanie had foolishly thought she needed to be independent, that it would be good for her to raise Macy on her own.

She hadn't realized how difficult it would be.

Things would be easier in Miami. She could build a nice life there. Dad would help watch Macy while she worked toward her master's degree.

Except she'd made the plans before she'd factored Tom into her future…

Macy yawned, and Stephanie hummed. Maybe Macy would fall asleep early. Stacks of folders, books and binders waited on the dining table.

She was tired of homework. And the rush, rush of each day. Get up, shower, slap some makeup on, get Macy dressed, throw a bagel in the toaster, race to day care, then to work. Classes three afternoons. Pick Macy up, stop at the store and spend fifteen minutes trying to figure out dinner, read a picture book, homework, guilt trip about not playing dolls and pass out in bed.

Stephanie closed her eyes a moment. Her life hadn't always been this hectic. The first months of marriage had been downright leisurely. She'd quit college right after getting engaged. With no real career goals and a low GPA from dropped classes, there didn't seem to be much point. And she'd had Tom to provide for her.

Ambitious. Driven.

But he'd been tender, protective and…

Absent.

No. No. No.

Pointless to entertain these feelings. Better to focus on the present.

Macy's breaths came in even intervals, so Stephanie carried her to the bedroom, tucked her in and plodded back to the dining room. Her ribs started aching again.

What to tackle first? The spreadsheet or the research paper? She pressed her fingers against her side, pulled a chair out, propped her elbows on the table and let her chin fall to her cradled hands. Who could focus on a stupid report after seeing him? The man she'd loved, the one she'd vowed to spend the rest of her life with. For better or for worse.

She'd been such a fool at twenty-one. If she had poured her energy into Tom instead of— well, she didn't want to think about it—maybe she wouldn't have had to spend the previous years alone, broke and exhausted.

But then there was the God factor. Maybe being at her lowest had finally allowed her to put her hope in Him. How many times had she read in Romans that God works for the good of those who love Him? And how many times did she have to remind herself she didn't have to earn His goodness? It was there for her simply because she trusted in Jesus as her Savior.

With the Lord's help, she'd create a future worthy of Macy.

Now that Tom was in the picture, how would their lives be affected? She hadn't been sure he'd want to be a father—a real father—to Macy. But he obviously did. Could she count on him to be involved in Macy's life, or would he come and go as it suited him?

He'd stood Stephanie up for countless dates during their brief marriage. How many meals had she eaten alone? When she married Tom, she'd never guessed he'd treat her the way her own mother did—unimportant. An accessory to his life.

It hurt. She squeezed her eyes shut. Still hurt.

If Tom wanted to be a father, he'd better commit all the way. If he broke Macy's heart…

She was getting ahead of herself. She didn't know his plans. Besides, Macy deserved to know who her dad was. But how should they break the news to her? And when?

"What do you mean you have a daughter?" Dad stopped pacing and spun to face Tom.

"What I said. I have a daughter." Tom extended his arm across the back of the tan couch. He'd called Dad and driven straight to Granddad's cottage from McDonald's. "Imagine how I felt coming home from my run and finding Stephanie, all bruised up, on my porch."

"A car accident, you said? She's okay?"

"Yeah."

Dad shook his head slowly, opened his mouth to speak, shut it and snapped his attention to Tom. "I'm a grandfather."

"You sure are."

"I have a granddaughter." Wonder filled his tone. Tom nodded, completely understanding his father's reaction. "Before I get too ahead of myself, Tommy, we need to consider a few things. I don't know how to put this…but given what you told us about…well, you know, how can you be sure the girl is yours?"

"I'm sure. Stephanie didn't cheat on me. I refused to believe her back then, told myself she wanted a future with that other guy, but I was wrong." Tom crossed to the large picture window with its endless views of the lake lined with evergreens. The familiar landscape of his childhood grounded him. Filled him with resolve he'd lacked earlier. "Macy looks just like me. Undeniable. The eyes. She's mine."

"She's got the Sheffield eyes? Imagine that." Dad jingled his key ring. His Carhartt jacket, faded baggy jeans and work boots gave him the appearance of a man in his early fifties, not his midsixties. Even his thick silver hair didn't age him. The man projected energy in motion at all times. "How old did you say she was?"

"Four." Tom wiped his hand over the back of his neck. The rawness of his discovery had choked him up off and on for the past hour.

"I'm sorry, Tommy. This must be hard to take in. Are you happy about it? At all?"

The concern in his eyes strangled Tom's throat even more. He coughed. "Yeah, Dad, I'm happy. I mean, a daughter—my daughter. It's…hard to describe. When I looked at her face and saw how small and cute she was, all I wanted to do was pick her up, buy her the contents of a toy store and protect her from everything that could hurt her. I can't explain. It was instant."

"Good. That's the way it's meant to be." Dad nodded. "What did you say her name was?"

"Macy."

"Macy." Dad tilted his head to the side. "You know she needs you, right? She needs her father."

"I know." The revelations had worn him out, and Tom returned to the couch, his legs splaying and his neck falling back against the cushions. "I still can't believe Stephanie kept this from me."

"I can't, either." Dad perched on the arm of the chair.

"How could she?" The loss of time with Macy hit him again. "How could she not tell me? I've been walking around in a daze all these years when I could have been spending time with my daughter."

All the wasted weekends, the boring nights, the hours at work—the aimless battery inside him that could have been sparked. If only he'd known.

"It's hard to understand. It will be harder to forgive."

Tom let out a dry laugh. "Forgive her? I can't. This is—"

"The hardest thing you'll have to do." Dad leveled the you-know-I'm-right stare he'd perfected years ago. Tom shifted his jaw but listened. "I'm not saying forgiveness has to happen immediately, but anger and bitterness won't help Macy.

Take my advice and give this to God as soon as possible or it will eat you alive."

It was already eating him alive. And he knew all about regrets and the way they hollowed a person out. The day he'd signed the divorce papers had set in motion a chain of choices he regretted as much as his brief marriage. Now Stephanie and her secrets flooded him with the past he'd fought hard to forget.

"I mean it, Tommy."

"You don't know what you're asking."

"I know exactly what I'm asking. Forgiving isn't pretending she didn't hurt you. I'm not saying you act like nothing happened. Pray for her. Pray for the mother of your child."

Tom shook his head. His neck was so tight, one more problem and it would snap.

Dad rose, his hand tapping against his thigh. "Do you want what's best for Macy?"

"Of course." He glared at him.

"Then find a way to forgive her mother."

Tom jumped to his feet, his fists balled at his sides. "She didn't think about me—did she, Dad? It's common knowledge you don't see other guys when you're married!"

Dad moved closer and looked him in the eye. "I'm not taking her side. You have the right to be angry with her. She hurt you. But for Macy's sake, you'll have to work on a civil relationship.

I don't know what Stephanie is like anymore, but when you two got married, I saw an insecure girl who had never heard of Jesus and didn't want to. I prayed for her then. I'm praying for her now."

Tom ground his teeth together. He spent enough time with his worn Bible each night to know that what Dad said made sense. But it didn't change the past. Tom would never get those early years with Macy back.

"She robbed me. She robbed me of my daughter. She robbed me of our marriage. You go ahead and pray for her. I'm not." Even as he said it, Stephanie's bruised face from earlier came to mind. The way she stood tall and maintained eye contact. Confidence infused her that hadn't been there before.

The front door opened and his sister Claire breezed inside. "This is a treat. You got here early for once."

Got here early? No. It couldn't be Tuesday.

Dinner at the cottage. With the family.

"Uh," Tom said, grabbing his keys. "I got to go."

"No. You backed out last week. You're staying." She set a huge orange Tupperware bowl on the table. "Besides, Reed and I have barely seen you lately. How's the training going?"

"Fine." If he made a break for it, he might be

able to skip dinner. But he stayed rooted. "It's going fine."

"Are you going to tell her or am I?" Dad raised his hands in a gesture of surrender. "I can't keep a secret to save my life."

Tom's insides shriveled. It was true. Dad *couldn't* keep a secret. He'd blown Sam's surprise birthday party a mere two months ago. But...tell everyone? Tonight? After the divorce, his siblings had treated him like a trauma patient for months. Did Tom really want to blab the news now?

"What's going on?" Claire raised an eyebrow. "You two are acting weird."

If he didn't say it, Dad would. Tom sighed. "I've got some news."

"What kind of news?" Wariness hung on her words.

"It's about Stephanie."

"Are you two getting back together?" She might as well have asked if he was sacrificing animals on the weekend.

"No. Nope." He shook his head. "No."

She exhaled loudly, her hand dropping from her lips to her chest. "Oh."

He furrowed his forehead. That's how his family viewed Stephanie—as someone Tom should avoid. And why wouldn't they? He'd bad-mouthed her enough after she left him. Not five minutes ago he'd smeared her past to his dad. He shouldn't have. He'd worked hard to overcome the bitterness, to own up to his part in their botched relationship.

And the tenderness in Stephanie's voice when she spoke of Macy, the way she'd tucked Macy's hair behind her ear at McDonald's, the fact she'd finally told him he had a daughter? It all tempted him to defend her. Which made no sense. One minute he was furious with her, and now he wanted to shield her?

"I found out—"

"Who's ready to eat?" Aunt Sally and the rest of the family entered the cottage in their usual noisy fashion. His brother and roommate, Bryan, two years younger than him, then their baby sister, Libby, chattered behind her husband, Jake. His youngest brother, Sam, zoomed straight to the living room and claimed the remote. Claire glided over to her husband, Reed, when he came in. And last but not least, Uncle Joe heaved warmers of food into the kitchen. The large, open living room and kitchen had high ceilings, hardwood floors and comfortable furniture. Felt like home. When Granddad was alive, it practically was home.

Good a place as any to make an announcement. Macy would be part of their lives, too. This cottage, this family—she was part of the Sheffields, and he'd make sure she knew it.

Tom cleared his throat and raised his arms.

Everyone turned to him. "Before we eat, I have something to tell you."

"Can't it wait until after Aunt Sally's chicken?" Sam yelled from the couch.

Grinning, Aunt Sally waved her hand. "Let the boy talk."

The boy. Tom had turned thirty-one this summer. Hardly a boy. His family continued to call him by his childhood nickname, Tommy, although he'd politely reminded them for years that his name was Tom.

"Go ahead, son." Dad gave a firm nod.

Words chased each other around his brain. "I saw Stephanie earlier."

"What? If you say you're getting back together with her…" Libby popped a hand on her hip, her blond ponytail swishing in the process.

"No, I'm not getting back with her." He glared at her. "She was in a car accident, and she came to the house. She told me…" He searched the sea of faces, full of questions, mostly encouraging, and his mouth went dry. His fingers curled around the edge of a dining chair. "I have a daughter."

A collective gasp filled the air, then hung there until complete silence suffocated the room.

"A little girl?" Aunt Sally's expression morphed from shocked to deliriously happy. "Did you hear that, everyone? We have a baby to spoil!"

Picking up on her cue, everyone murmured

and nodded, although not nearly as enthusiastic as his aunt.

Dad clapped for silence. "I, for one, can't wait to meet her." He turned to face Tom. "We'll do everything we can to support you and help out."

His siblings rushed to him.

"When did you find out?" Bryan asked.

"A few hours ago," Tom said.

"And you're just accepting her word on this?" Bryan's tone was accusing.

He drew his shoulders back. "If you have something to say, say it."

"She ruined your life once, and what do you know? She's found a way to ruin it again."

"I don't consider finding out I have a daughter to be ruining my life."

Bryan shrugged. "Whatever, man. I'm trying to look out for you."

"Congratulations." Sam jostled between them. "I think."

Libby bumped Sam to the side. "Are you kidding me? I am this close—" she held her finger and thumb a sliver away from each other "—to hunting Stephanie down and telling her what I think—"

"Libby." Jake tugged on her arm. "Not the time or place."

She clamped her mouth shut, eyelashes reaching to the ceiling. "Fine."

Aunt Sally threw her arms around Tom. Then she stepped back and placed her hands on his cheeks, her dangling pumpkin earrings jingling as she grinned. "I'm thanking God extra tonight that He's led you to your baby. What a blessing."

The truth of her statement hit him like a kettle-bell to the chest. "It is a blessing, isn't it?"

"The circumstances are less than ideal. I know. I know." She patted his cheek. "I've had bitter times. They can eat away at your soul. As hard as it might be, I hope you'll try to focus on the positive. What's the little sweetheart's name?"

"Macy."

"Macy," she said, tears forming in her eyes. "What a pretty name. I'm going shopping tomorrow to buy her some outfits." She drew her palms together. "I'll just guess at the sizes."

"She's four and about this tall." Tom held his hand above his knee. "If that helps."

She winked. "It does."

A yank on his arm got his attention. Claire. "Come on." She pulled him out to the deck, where the sun had dropped to a glowing mound on the horizon.

Bryan followed them. "Is this a private conversation?" Attitude cut through each word.

Tom's jaw tightened as he peered at Claire, concerned, then Bryan, livid. "Don't act like a baby." He stalked over to the deck rail and peered out at the darkening sky. "I don't know what to do."

The sliding door swooshed, and Libby and Sam joined them.

"Of all the rotten things she did to you, this is the worst. I'm shocked, but I shouldn't be." Libby drew herself to her full height and shook her head.

"Libby," Claire warned.

"What?" She turned to Tom. "What if she's trying to milk you for child support?"

"She didn't even want me to know."

"Oh, that's so much better."

"Shut up, Libby," Bryan said.

"Tell us about your daughter." Claire's smile was encouraging.

Tom stretched his neck to one side, then the other. He might as well get the basics out of the way. "She's four. Looks just like me. She's smart, too. Maybe even a genius."

"I can't wait to meet her," Claire said.

"Since no one else is willing to state the obvious, I will." Libby jutted her chin out. "Why now? Why did Stephanie decide to tell you today? After all this time? I'll tell you why. Money. Or babysitting. She's going to start calling you nonstop, wanting you to watch the kid for her. And then she'll want you back."

Libby was wrong. Whatever Stephanie wanted

wasn't free babysitting or child support. But Libby did raise a good point. What were Stephanie's expectations for him as a father? He wanted to spend time getting to know his daughter—gradually. His training schedule didn't leave much room. After Christmas, he'd really have to kick it in gear with swimming at the Y and adding miles to his runs each week.

What was he thinking? No race was worth more than his daughter.

Slipping back into mediocrity already.

Not fair. Who said he couldn't be a dad and have a life? He'd find a way to get to know Macy *and* train for the race.

"Stephanie wasn't an ogre, Libby." Claire steepled her fingers, keeping her tone even. "She made mistakes. We all do."

"But her mistakes hurt Tommy." Libby crossed her arms over her chest.

Tom held his hands up. "I don't know why she finally told me." The words weren't easier to say this time. "The accident shook her up. It's no secret we weren't right for each other." Or, rather, he wasn't right for her. How many times had he replayed their relationship in his mind, trying to figure out how he could have done it all differently?

"That's a bunch of baloney." Libby shook her head. "Half the women in this county would rob the Snack-N-Go to have a shot at marrying you. She blew it."

"I blew it, too, Libs." It was the first time he'd admitted it out loud. Over the years, he'd accepted his responsibility in their divorce, but he'd never told anyone. Stephanie's confession gave him the courage to make his own. "She wasn't the only one to blame. You know the saying 'It takes two'? In our case, it's true."

The breeze made a shushing noise in the trees, and Bryan moved to stand beside him. "What are you going to do now?"

Tom lifted one shoulder. "I don't know."

"You fighting for custody?" Bryan asked.

"I'm not going to walk away, if that's what you're asking. But I...don't know."

"You'll figure it out," Claire said. "You'll be a terrific dad."

"You know what this means," Sam said. "You'll be in Stephanie's life again."

Tom fought a wave of helplessness, the same feeling that kept gushing up when he thought about spending time with Macy. Sam was right. He wouldn't be able to avoid Stephanie. Was he ready to be a part of her life again? Especially not as her husband? What if she was dating some-one? He had limits, and being a bystander to his ex-wife's love life went way beyond them. Seeing her again, being near her…messed with his resolve to protect his heart.

"Hey." Claire placed her hand on his sleeve. "Don't worry. I'm going to pray hard for you. I'm upset you're finding out about Macy now, but you're a dad. That's good! I can't wait to meet this little girl. I know she'll be fabulous. She has our genes, right?"

He straightened, not knowing what to say. Dusk blanketed them, and lights across the lake popped on, reflecting thin beams zigzagging on the water. Each of his siblings' faces turned to him with varying expressions. Claire, tender and concerned. Sam, indifferent. Libby, skeptical, and Bryan, fierce.

"Whatever you need," Claire said. "We're here for you."

His phone vibrated in his pocket. He checked the number. Didn't recognize it. "Hello?"

"Tom?" Stephanie's voice rang through. "Do you think you could come over tomorrow?"

Tom pressed the intercom and shifted the enormous white stuffed rabbit complete with pink bow to his other arm. The old apartment complex a mile from campus didn't exactly look seedy, but brown paint peeled from the exterior, bare spots riddled the patches of grass and potholes and cracks dismembered the pavement. He shifted his jaw. College students didn't mill about—a relief—but the junky cars had him questioning the neighbors. Was his daughter safe living here? Was Stephanie?

The door buzzed, and he stepped inside. Soiled, worn indoor/outdoor carpet greeted him. A half flight of stairs stood at his right, a hallway with closed doors to his left. The scent of laundry detergent mingled with spices—foreign, curry? He climbed the stairs, turned, jogged up another set and landed on the third floor.

Stephanie ushered him inside. "Thanks for coming." She dead-bolted the door behind him and nodded at the stuffed animal. "Macy will love this. Why don't you have a seat?"

She waved to the small living room to his right. White walls, an old forest green couch, an upholstered rocking chair covered with a quilt and a bin of toys furnished the room. Lamps glowed, and the end tables held neat stacks of children's books. Sheer curtains flanked a glass door leading to a balcony. Not luxurious but welcoming enough.

"Can I get you something to drink?" She flitted to the tiny kitchen and opened the fridge. Her jeans and slouchy lavender sweater made her appear younger, more beautiful than he remembered. Or was it her expression? The Stephanie who'd walked out on him rarely smiled, always nibbled on the corner of her lip and had a nervous air. This woman reminded him of the Steph he fell in love with.

Don't go there. Focus on now. On Macy.

"Water would be good." He set the bunny on the floor and lowered his tall frame onto the couch. "Where's Macy?"

She returned with two glasses of ice water and set one on a coaster next to him before sitting in the rocking chair and tucking one foot under her body. "She's still at day care. I wanted to talk to you in private."

Warmth pooled through his core. She wanted to talk to him? In private? He straightened and shifted forward. "What about?"

A crease grew in her forehead. "Isn't it obvious?"

Libby's words sang in his mind, *She's going to start calling you nonstop. She'll want you back.* The thought wasn't as unwelcome as it should be.

"I guess I thought…" She blinked twice. Enticing brown eyes. "You acted like you wanted to get to know Macy."

His jaw relaxed. *Dummy.* Stephanie didn't want him—still didn't want him. "I do."

"Of course."

Was she disappointed? If yes, why had she invited him over?

She stood next to the balcony door, staring outside. "I don't want Macy to be caught in our problems the way I was with Mom and her husbands."

"Well, I'm not like them."

"True." She tapped her chin with her finger. "From my experience, though, lots of adults don't think about their kids in these situations. They give in to their petty dramas, not caring who they hurt. I'd move mountains to protect Macy."

"So I didn't even get a chance?"

"We've been over this. Your parting words, the whiplash speed of the divorce papers and my own experience in a split home forced me to make a decision. The wrong one, obviously."

Tom stared at a stain in the carpet. The night she left rushed back. He could still feel the blood churning in his veins. Tears streaked her face as she told him there was nothing between her and that guy, that she wasn't cheating and would never cheat on him. But his vision had blurred and all he could see was her holding hands with the jerk. He'd lost all trust in her. Refused marriage counseling. Rushed to the lawyer for a divorce.

Hotheaded. Since then he'd worked hard to tame his impulsive side.

She picked at her sleeve. "I know what it's like to be neglected by a parent who doesn't want you."

"You think I would neglect my own child?" he asked quietly.

"I don't know. Honestly, Tom, I felt very neglected in our marriage."

He grabbed the glass of water and drank. It didn't surprise him to hear those words, but they hurt. The truth hurt.

"Macy's my whole world," she said. "It hasn't been easy doing this on my own."

The sadness in her eyes tore at his conscience, but sympathizing would get him in trouble. The kind of trouble that started with forgiveness and ended with… "That was your choice. To do it on your own."

"You act like I wanted to get pregnant and live with my dad."

A retort begged to come out, but he counted to three. "Well, what's done is done. I want to tell Macy I'm her dad. I'm ready to be her father now."

"This isn't all about you. Think about her."

He leaned back, at a complete loss for words. He had agreed to her charade last night, and now she wanted to continue it? Not going to happen. If she refused to bend about this, he'd call his lawyer. Work out a visitation schedule where he could have Macy to himself.

"I don't know what kind of game you're playing, but I pass." He stood, flexing his hands.

"I'm Macy's father. I'm telling her, I'm spending time with her and there's nothing you can do to stop me."

Chapter Three

"Wait. Tom—" Stephanie rushed to him, blocking his path.

What was wrong with her? She knew better than to come out guns firing, and yet she had. If she wasn't careful, blame would get tossed back and forth like a twisted game of hot potato. She summoned every ounce of patience and lifted her chin.

"Please sit down." She sighed. "I didn't call you here to fight. And I don't expect you to believe it, but I've changed. Part of that change has been trying to become someone trustworthy."

He lifted his eyebrows but sat.

"Before you take matters into your hands," she continued, "would you agree to spend some time with Macy first?"

"Is this a trick?" His gaze dropped to the stuffed bunny.

"No, it's not a trick. Think about it." She smoothed her sweater over her hips. Tom didn't know Macy, didn't know she sang "I Am Jesus' Little Lamb" before bed each night, loved noodles, hated peas, refused to wear socks with stripes and wouldn't brush her teeth unless she could use her Oscar the Grouch toothbrush. Learning those details took time.

"Why should I?" he asked.

Of all the clueless things to say. The response was so Tom, she had to bite back a retort. But she wasn't surprised. He wanted his daughter now, whether Macy was ready or not. Why would he bother to get to know anyone—his daughter included—when he'd made zero effort to get to know his own wife?

Stephanie returned to the chair and sat. "It would be easier if she felt comfortable with you before telling her you're her dad." She waited for him to disagree and storm out, but he lifted his gaze to hers. Nervous. Scared?

Impossible. Not him.

"I think you're right." He grimaced, ducking his chin.

Wait, had he just told her she was right? She almost did a double take.

"Good," she said. "I don't think it will take long, either. She's a wonderful girl."

"I know she is." His chest puffed out.

Another surprise. Tom already put Macy on a pedestal. Stephanie's heart lifted a little at the thought. Sharing Macy with Tom wouldn't be horrible if Stephanie knew her baby was loved. But she still had a lot of questions to clear up first. "If we're going to do this, we should probably catch up so there aren't any misunderstandings."

Tom frowned. "What do you mean?"

"Um." She opened her palms, unsure how to continue. "I guess we should know what we're getting into, like get up to speed on each other's lives. What's your schedule like? Do you have a girlfriend? That sort of thing."

The look on his face screamed "get me out of here." She quickly continued, "I'll start it off. I work full-time as a receptionist for a dentist nearby, and I'll have my bachelor degree in accounting this spring. I plan on getting my master's degree, too. I...actually, I—" She stalled, not ready to mention Florida. Hadn't Dad always warned her not to poke the bear? She'd wait to tell Tom, when they could spend at least five minutes being civil to each other.

"Are you trying to tell me you have a boyfriend?" He barked out the words, but he didn't seem angry. No, the way he flicked his thumb against his finger wasn't anger. She'd seen Tom in many moods, but this wasn't one of them. She peeked at his hands again. Could he be vulnerable?

With a quick shake of her head, she said, "No."

"What is it, then?" He met her eyes, and she got lost in their beauty. *Look away!*

One thing Tom had always pressured her to do when they were married was attend church with him, but she never had. Not once. She wasn't ready to share her Florida plans yet, but maybe Tom deserved to know about more than just her career plans and nonexistent love life. "I'm a believer now. Been attending church for two years. Macy, too."

"Really?"

"Yeah. Turns out you were right. I needed a savior." She shuddered to think what her life would be like without God. He got her through each day, filled her with peace when life got chaotic, comforted her when she doubted her actions.

He lightly clasped his hands in his lap. "Don't we all."

They stared at each other a moment, a ray of understanding between them. The man on her couch resembled the Tom she'd married, but he seemed more complex. Tempted her to unravel the mystery and find out who he'd become. She shook her head. Good thing she'd earned a black belt in avoiding temptation.

"While we're putting our lives out there, I need to know something." He cleared his throat, lowered his gaze. "Has Macy had a man in her life?"

"Just my dad." She blinked. "No boyfriends."

"What about, well, you know?"

"Aaron?" She waved dismissively. "No. I don't expect you to believe this, but when you confronted me about him, it changed my life."

"It changed mine, too." His gruff tone filled the air. She wanted to touch him, comfort him. But she'd forfeited that right years ago.

"I saw Aaron for what he was—a lonely, insecure guy who got a kick out of pursuing an off-limits woman. And I guess I saw myself for what I was, too. I'd been playing the victim. I needed to take responsibility for my life. I don't blame you for hating me. And I don't expect you to ever forgive me."

"I told you I don't hate you. It's been a long time. I'm over it."

"Good." She tried to smile, but her heart caved in. It shouldn't hurt, hearing his dismissal, but it did. "Have you found someone new?"

"No." He shook his head. "The single life is for me."

She blew out a breath, relief trickling to her gut. He *was* single. Not that it meant anything to her—it was just better for Macy. Stephanie couldn't handle the thought of a jealous girlfriend making Macy miserable. Although, a woman getting close to her daughter left a sour taste in her mouth, too. Complications piled up in her mind. She tossed them away. "Still working at the dealership?"

He nodded. "I own two of them."

"Good for you." *Two dealerships. Twice the amount of work. Double the hours?* She hoped not.

Silence lingered, made her fidget. What else was there to say? A lot, actually, but none of it really mattered. Except the one thing she hadn't yet clarified. The one thing Tom was bound to fight her on.

"So, I have an idea how we can do this." She drew her palms together, her chin resting on her fingertips.

He narrowed his eyes. "Do what?"

"Spend time together—the three of us—to make Macy feel comfortable with you."

His lips tugged downward as if he'd bitten into a Sour Patch Kids candy. "The three of us?"

"Until she's used to you. Then we can figure out a way to tell her you're her dad. Work out a visitation schedule."

She waited for his outburst, his objection. He stared at the window a moment, then met her eyes.

"Okay, but I'm not waiting forever." He raked his hand through his hair. "How does Saturday afternoon work for you?"

* * *

Ridiculous.

He'd accepted her terms without a fight. Tom merged his truck onto the highway, cranking a Keith Urban song louder.

Who was he kidding? All the fight had left him when she'd walked out five years ago. It had happened so quickly. They'd met, gotten engaged, been married and divorced in just over a year. He'd been coasting ever since.

Not true. He'd stopped drifting when he'd started training. He pressed on the accelerator. He'd already added three miles to his hardest runs. Given up pop and junk food. This race was worth pushing himself for. It had to be.

Years of being stuck in the past, of being convinced he wasn't enough, had taken its toll. Regrets and blame roared through his gut. The blame he'd gotten through with the help of his Bible. But the regrets?

He hadn't been a good husband. So wrapped up in his new responsibilities of managing Dad's car dealership, he'd worked seventy-hour weeks and ignored his bride. She was right about that. He *had* neglected her.

He'd loved her. And he'd blown it. Hadn't paid attention to the signs, but in hindsight, they'd been there. She'd cooked special meals he never showed up for. Worse, he'd barely thanked her.

And, on more than one occasion, he'd lost track of time reviewing reports when he was supposed to meet her at a restaurant or the movies. He'd ignored her sadness and basically acted as if marriage was all about him.

It didn't excuse her, though. She'd lied, went behind his back and gotten close with another guy. But what had she said just now? About seeing that jerk for who he was—a lonely scuzzball? Maybe she hadn't put it in those words, but she might as well have. He grinned for a moment, and then a slew of questions about his future assaulted him.

The exit he normally took came and went, and within minutes he found himself at the zoo gate where Claire worked. He texted her. Meet me out front? I need to talk.

He should be driving home, lacing up his shoes and hitting the pavement. Should be acting as if what happened today didn't matter. But a feeling of caving in, of losing—what, he didn't know— coursed through his body.

His phone dinged. I'll be there in five minutes.

Five minutes. Too long. The taste in his mouth turned to copper.

Maybe he hadn't caved in. And he certainly hadn't lost anything. He'd let Stephanie have her plan because...

He wasn't ready for this. He wasn't ready to be a dad.

"There you are." Claire sailed through the gate and gave him a hug. "How did it go? Did she love the bunny?"

"I'm not sure." He led Claire to a bench. Seeing her in the khaki pants and polo shirt with her name embroidered on it always filled him with pride. His sister had wanted to work for the zoo since she was a little kid. Her dream finally came true this year. Some people's dreams did anyway. "I didn't see her."

"What?" Claire's stricken face matched her tone. "Why?"

"Stephanie thinks we should ease Macy into this."

"Oh, like you get to know her before telling her you're her dad?"

He nodded. Claire made it sound reasonable.

"Makes sense to me," she added. "Does it bother you so much?"

"Not that. She wants to be there, too."

"Who? Stephanie?" The corners of her lip curled down and she shrugged. "Might be smart."

"You think so?" He clung to the thought.

"Yeah." She brushed a piece of straw off her pants. "Think about it. If you're a four-year-old girl, would you want to spend time with some strange man if your mom isn't around? You'd likely terrify her, no offense."

"None taken." He hadn't pursued that angle before. His apprehension lightened. "But it's hard."

"I know. It is hard. Spending time with your ex-wife is hard."

"I worry— Never mind." Spending time with Stephanie was difficult because she reminded him of the dreams he'd tucked away. Before they got married, he'd had a plan. Make the dealership a success, buy a house, start a family. Except he'd failed. He jerked his head to the side. The sun warmed his face. He didn't dare say what he was thinking out loud.

Claire touched his arm. "Are you worried about her hurting you again?"

How did Claire always cut to the heart of it? He nodded.

"Tommy, Aunt Sally once asked me if I believed I'm always divinely guided, and I told her yes. Do you know what she said to me after?"

He shook his head.

"She told me I would always take the right turn in the road. I believe that. Now you'll have to ask yourself the same question."

The clouds feathered across the sky as he pondered what she said. Divinely guided, yes. But did he always take the right turn in the road? No. He'd made too many wrong turns to believe it.

"I was kind of glad Stephanie suggested taking it slow. I'm not ready to be alone with my own kid. I have no idea what little girls like to do, what they need, what they eat. I'm clueless, Claire." Plus, he was drawn to Stephanie, not that he'd ever admit it. Would he get lost in another thankless relationship with her? Where he'd end up the loser again?

She laughed. "You're going to be great. Macy will love you. Just take lots of notes on how Stephanie handles things. And when you're in doubt, ask Macy what she likes."

He didn't voice the other concern spinning around his head. What if he spent time with them and realized he was a terrible dad? That Macy was better off without him in her life?

"Something else is on your mind," Claire said. "I can see it."

She knew him well, but he wasn't ready to confide in her. "I finally got the guts to sign up for something I'd been thinking about for years, and this situation could end it."

"You're not going to quit training. This race is too important to you, so don't even go there. We'll keep you on track. And I get you'd be nervous about…this situation—about Stephanie. You don't have to explain. You sprinted through the whole relationship, and she's, what, five years younger than you? You two weren't ready for marriage, and it's not as if you're dating again—

you're spending time together so you can be the dad you were meant to be."

The words sprinkled over him, shedding a layer of guilt he'd thought he'd eliminated. "Thanks, Claire." Hanging out with Stephanie and Macy would give him the skills he needed to be a good father. He'd have to keep reminding himself.

And if not?

He wouldn't think about it. He'd be a good parent. Period.

Claire grinned. "You realize what this means, right?"

He frowned. "No clue."

"You're going to have to break the news to Aunt Sally she won't be meeting Macy yet."

"Come on." Stephanie pulled Macy by the hand through the parking lot of Johnson's Pumpkin Patch Saturday afternoon. Cars and trucks crawled along the lane until a flagger directed them to park in a field. She scurried through the couples as best as she could.

Boy, it was busy. Laughter, conversation and the occasional squeal punctured the festive atmosphere. Attracted to the sweetness of the nearby apple trees, bees swarmed about the picnic tables she passed. The sun shone hot on her face, and she drank in the aroma of homemade doughnuts. Cinnamon. Her stomach grumbled.

Macy's hand began to slip from her fingers,

but she gripped it tighter. "We're late, so please walk faster."

"Why are we meeting *him* here, Mommy?" Macy whined, each step deliberately slow. Her sling tapped against her little chest to the rhythm of their movements. "Why didn't we come, just us?"

Stephanie inwardly sighed. Between working full-time, all the hours spent at school, then hunching over homework each evening, she understood why Macy clung to her when they were together. Even when they went to the park, Macy never ran off to play with other kids. She wanted her mom all to herself.

"Because it's good to have friends." Stephanie beamed. Maybe her lame answer would put a stop to more questions. If the guilt about not telling Tom was bad, the guilt about not giving Macy a father was worse.

"Don't want no more friends." Macy's knees inched higher as she marched.

"Don't be silly. Everyone wants friends. You like Tatum at preschool, right? And Josie at day care."

Macy dug her heels in and yanked back. *Now what?*

"You don't need more friends. You have me." Her glistening eyes pleaded with Stephanie.

She knelt and tweaked Macy's nose. "Of course

I have you. And we're best friends. But I'm your mom, too. And we both can have other friends."

"I don't like him." Her lower lip bulged.

"Why not?" Why would Macy already not like Tom? She'd seemed fine with him at McDonald's.

In her pink fleece jacket and pigtails riding high on her head, Macy bobbed her chin and scrunched her face up into a major pout. "I'm not going."

Stephanie straightened. Not now. A temper tantrum when they were already running late? Couldn't one thing in her life be easy? Just once?

"You are going." She put her stern tone on. "This isn't your decision. We're meeting Tom here, picking out pumpkins, and you will use your manners."

Macy stomped her foot.

"That is unacceptable, Macy. Do you hear me?"

Macy's nose soared, defiance radiating out of her.

Patience. Give me patience.

Might be time for a change of tactic. An act of desperation, surely, and not one any parenting expert would condone, but something had to be done. "I thought you wanted a doughnut. If you forget your manners, you will not get one."

"I want a doughnut!" Macy's eyes widened.

"Well, then, you'll have to behave."

A moment passed before Macy sighed. "Yes, Mommy."

Stephanie reached for her hand again. They hustled toward the big barn converted to a country store. Macy oohed over an orange cat running by, and Stephanie craned her neck to see through the clusters of people. Tom's tall, athletic frame rounded the corner, and her pulse thumped, then sped up. His easy smile? Just like when they first met. In a navy blue pullover and jeans, he attracted several female stares, yet he appeared oblivious to the admiration. She tightened her hold around Macy's hand.

"Ouch, Mommy."

"Sorry." All worked up over six feet of strapping male. And why not? They'd been good together, once upon a time.

He squatted in front of Macy, grinned and held out his hand. "I believe we met already, Miss Macy. How are you doing today? Are you ready to pick out a pumpkin?"

Macy hesitated, but she eventually shook his hand, her eyes stony.

"What's wrong? Don't you like pumpkins?" He righted himself to a standing position.

Stephanie nudged her.

"They're all right." Macy sounded as enthused as she did when she had to get a booster shot.

"Thanks for meeting us here, Tom." Stephanie plastered her widest smile on. "Why don't we mosey out to the field? Which patch is the best, do you think?"

With questions in his eyes, he glanced at Macy, who was now picking at her sling. "Looks like a lot of people are headed that way." He pointed to a lane where kids ran ahead, moms pushed strollers and dads toted young boys or girls on their shoulders.

"Do you want a ride, Macy?" He tapped his shoulders.

She shook her head, pigtails slapping the sides of her face.

"Okay." He frowned.

Stephanie considered pulling him aside to explain, but what could she say? *Macy isn't really a brat. She's acting like one because she doesn't want to share me.* Yeah, that would sound great. Stephanie did the best she could as a single mom, and sometimes it wasn't good enough. When she'd lived with Dad, it hadn't been as bad. He played with Macy while Stephanie tackled a term paper. He soothed the tension when her patience vanished.

She peeked at her daughter, clutching her hand. How would Tom fall in love with Macy if she acted like a sullen statue?

They made their way to the lane. Ducks flew

overhead in a V formation, and a line of trees swished in the light wind.

"So what have you been up to?" Stephanie forced a cheery tone. "How is your family?"

His sharp glance ratcheted her nerves. "They're good. Claire got married this summer, Libby earlier this year. Bryan and I run all the dealerships, and we share a house. Sam took over as CEO of Sheffield Auto last fall."

"Your dad retired?"

"Yes and no." He chuckled. "He retired from the auto business to be a superintendent for my brother-in-law. Dad is in construction now."

"I always liked Dale." She stepped over a tree root bumping out of the ground. "I could see him in construction. He's got a lot of energy."

"When my grandpa retired, he had a big party. He has lots of energy, too," Macy said with a shade of snottiness.

"Good." Tom nodded. "I'm sure he enjoyed his party."

"He did. We got him floaty balloons and everything." She picked up her pace, shoulders wiggling with her determined stride.

"I miss my grandpa. He taught me how to tie ropes and build birdhouses. We went out on his fishing boat all summer. I wish he was still around."

"Where did he go?" For the first time since arriving, her voice wasn't dripping with attitude.

"Heaven. He died a while back."

"I'm going to heaven, too." She jabbed her chest with her thumb. "My Sunday school teacher told me so."

Tom grinned down at her. The most patient, loving expression crossed his face. Stephanie almost gasped. Loving, yes. But patient? She sifted through her memories. He'd always been quick with a reply. Time must have mellowed him. But maybe that wasn't fair on her part. Could she say she truly knew him when they were only together a year?

He tugged one of Macy's pigtails. "Well, you keep listening to your Sunday school teacher."

"Mommy's going to heaven. Aren't you?"

"Yes. And Tom is, also."

"No, he's not." Macy shook her head and laughed.

"Macy, that's a very mean thing to say." Stephanie halted.

"But—"

"No buts. All believers go to heaven. You know that."

"You mean I have to share you there, too?" she wailed. "I don't want to go anymore."

Stephanie dreaded looking at Tom, but she had

to. His curious expression reassured her. "Will you excuse us a minute, please?"

He nodded.

She marched Macy to the side of the lane and kept her voice low. "Why did you say that, Macy? Do you know you hurt his feelings?"

"I don't care." Her cheeks drooped. "Heaven isn't for him. It's for us. It's our girl place."

"It's not our girl place. We will be together, but everyone else who trusted in God will, too. You wouldn't want to leave anyone out of heaven, would you?"

Macy bowed her head and dragged her tennis shoe back and forth in the dirt.

"Answer me, Macy."

"I want to go home."

Clenching her hands into fists, Stephanie waited until her nerves calmed before answering. "Fine. I'll take you home. I'll call the sitter. You can stay there, but I'm coming back to pick out pumpkins with Tom."

That got her attention. Macy wrapped her arms around Stephanie's legs. "No! I want to stay. He can go to heaven, too."

"It's not your decision if he goes to heaven or not. You owe him an apology."

"But, Mama—"

"No buts." Stephanie led Macy back to the lane. "Macy has something to say to you. Don't you?"

"I'm sorry." The muffled words barely were out before she started sobbing.

Stephanie wrapped her in a hug and kissed her head. "I know apologizing was hard, but you did the right thing."

Macy pulled away and wiped her eyes. "Do I still get a doughnut?"

"It depends." Stephanie darted a glance Tom's way and mouthed, "Sorry." Then she moved forward. "Let's try over there. I see a big pumpkin with your name all over it."

Chapter Four

Thankfully, her lunch break had finally arrived. The phones had been ringing nonstop all morning, and if Stephanie had to argue with one more insurance rep about covering a porcelain filling, she was going to rip the phone out of the wall. There wasn't enough chocolate in the world for Mondays like this.

Bea, the other receptionist at the dentist office, had invited her to eat at their favorite deli. As they crossed the parking lot to get into Bea's sporty black car, Bea chatted about her upcoming vacation plans.

"You sure have been quiet. Are you feeling okay?" Bea asked. Her chic white bob and subtle makeup matched her warm, intelligent personality. Stephanie considered her more of a worldly-wise aunt than a coworker.

"I'm fine. A little stressed." As the car merged

with traffic, Stephanie relaxed into the seat. At least the sun was shining. The day wasn't completely bad. "Every time I answer the phone it's a crisis."

"Tell me about it." She chuckled and peeked over. "A little green is peeking out from your bruise again. Remind me to touch it up with my concealer stick when we return." She braked for a traffic light. "What are you going to do about your car?"

"Insurance is supposed to cut me a check this week. My old one wasn't worth much, so I'll have to find a used car in a limited price range." Another to-do on an already crowded list. If only Dad was here. He'd help her pick out a vehicle. He'd check it over and tell her if it had major problems. She missed him. Missed having someone to rely on.

"How's Macy doing?"

"Her wrist hurts, but she's convinced she doesn't need the sling. You know how kids are." They sped past apartment buildings, fast-food joints, the pharmacy and a grocery store before coming to a stop at the bustling sandwich shop.

Since moving to Kalamazoo, Stephanie hadn't told anyone about Tom, but she longed to confide in someone. And she appreciated Bea's faith-filled perspective, something Dad lacked. She'd tried to get him to attend church with her, but he'd never been interested. Moving here and meeting Bea had given her a Christian shoulder to cry on, not that she did very often. But now she needed help—emotional and advice-wise.

After ordering subs and sodas, they found a table in the corner next to a window. Bea opened her sandwich to look it over before taking a bite, but Stephanie left hers wrapped next to her.

"I have to tell you something, and I'm really nervous about it." Stephanie folded her hands, clutching them tightly. Questions swirled in Bea's hazel eyes. "I think we're good enough friends that you won't hold this against me, but if you don't want to talk to me after this, I understand."

"We're not in high school." Bea flung a stray onion off her cheese, closed the bun and bit into it. "Nothing you could say would kill our friendship. I've done things I'm not proud of."

Nothing like this. Stephanie drew her shoulders back. "I used to be married. Five years ago, to be exact. The whole romance whizzed by quicker than a Michigan spring. Within six months of saying 'I do,' we split up. During the divorce, I found out I was pregnant, but the way things ended...I didn't think he'd ever want to see me again."

Bea's sandwich hovered next to her mouth. Stephanie didn't know what to say. Then Bea blinked and made a rolling gesture with her arm. "Well, go on."

Her teeth chattered. "Everything fell apart that year. I dropped out of school before the wedding. My college friends—the same ones I'd had all through high school—wanted me to hang out and party with them. Tom was working his way up at his dad's company and had no time for me. I spent more and more evenings with my friends and their friends, and one friend in particular. He listened. Looked at me like I was somebody. Made me feel less lonely. We started meeting on our own. I justified it, telling myself Tom wasn't paying attention to me, that it didn't hurt anyone because we were just talking. But Tom drove into the city one day, and he saw us holding hands."

Bea set her food on the table and leaned forward.

"He confronted me that night, and I finally, finally told him about Aaron. And I felt like nothing. Less than nothing. The truth slapped me in the face. I was indulging in an emotional affair. Tom and I got into a terrible fight. I packed a suitcase and drove to my dad's. When I called him a few days later, I suggested counseling, but he refused and had divorce papers drawn up the next week."

"And then you found out about Macy?"

Stephanie nodded. "I never told him about her."

"Because you thought Tom hated you and never wanted to see you again," Bea said. "You probably hated yourself a little, too, didn't you?"

Tears pressed against the backs of her eyes. "Yeah," she whispered. "I did."

"Honey, I know you." Bea covered Stephanie's hand with her own. "I see how devoted you are to Macy. Are you thinking about telling him now? Did the accident shake you up?"

The accident had shaken her up, all right. "He already knows."

"What? I'm confused. How?"

"I drove to his house last week and spilled everything."

Bea's eyebrows shot up.

"I couldn't live with the guilt another minute. And my conscience has been churning overtime. I can't explain it. When I go to church, I feel blessed and convicted at the same time."

"Consciences have a way of doing that. Didn't you say you're a relatively new believer?"

"Yeah." Stephanie peered at the ceiling a moment. "It's been about two years, I guess. When Macy was a toddler, she got sick. Really sick. With scarlet fever. As her temperature rose, a rash appeared. She just sat there, listless. It scared me. I thought of Tom's family, how church seemed to sustain them, how they talked about God like He was a real father."

"That's right," Bea murmured.

Stephanie attempted a smile. "I prayed. Day and night, I prayed. I gave my problems to God. It was the first time I felt peace, real peace, you know. The second round of antibiotics cured Macy. Going to church strengthened my faith, and I knew I should tell Tom, but I didn't have the courage. He'd flat out told me he was glad we never had kids. I worried if I told him, he'd reject her because of me. The guilt grew and grew."

"Guilt's like a virus, spreading unless we tame it."

Stephanie sniffed. "Anyway, the accident woke me up. Macy has been asking—she deserves to know who her father is. And Tom should have been told from day one. What if something happens to me? Dad won't live forever."

"How did—Tom, is it?—take the news?"

Stephanie traced the rim of her soda. "Surprisingly well. He actually acts thrilled to be a dad. He probably won't ever forgive me, not that I blame him, but he embraced the idea of having a child."

"Given what happened with what's-his-name, did he question if she's his?"

"Oh, yeah, but Macy is Tom's mirror image. All I had to do was show him a picture. No question."

"So what are you two going to do now?"

"I asked him to ease her into it. She thinks he's an old friend."

"Good." Bea nodded. "So he seems interested, like he wants to be part of her life. That's encouraging."

"Looks that way." She unwrapped her sub, although her stomach dry-heaved at the thought of eating. If she didn't, she'd never make it through class this afternoon.

"So what happened to the other guy?"

Stephanie lifted one shoulder. "I truly loved Tom. When it came down to it, Aaron lacked integrity. And so did I."

"You're a good mom, Stephanie. You should be proud of yourself."

She swallowed the lump in her throat. "Thank you. I… I might be a better person now, but I still have to pay."

"I don't know about that." Bea lifted her sandwich again. "I'd say you already paid a high price for your past. If Tom is willing to be a father for Macy, you'd be smart to let him. Every girl needs a daddy."

"I know, I know. I'm just scared. I've had her all to myself. Now I have to share her? What if he sues for custody?"

Bea leveled a firm stare her way. "Then you'd be smart to make this as easy as possible for him. Accommodate him. Be the person you wanted to be when you were married. Show him you've changed—if you don't..."

Stephanie crinkled her nose. "What?"

"Well, a father who resents his child's mother isn't ideal."

Stephanie hadn't thought of that. She'd assumed... What had she assumed? Tom would take the high road? When she'd taken the low road? Would he want revenge? No, he'd never poison their daughter's thoughts against her. Not Tom.

She pushed her hair from her face, wincing as her thumb touched her bruised cheek.

"You okay?" Bea asked. "It's a lot to think about, but don't get tempted to go down the worst-scenario road. Handle this maturely, and the outcome will be good, not bad."

"Mature?" She almost choked. "I'm trying. I don't know if I can handle this."

"You can call me anytime. And keep praying," Bea said. "Maybe God has something wonderful planned with all this."

Something wonderful? Those kinds of things happened to people who didn't lie and hurt others. Which left her out. No matter how much she tried to make up for the past, she couldn't.

"Have you forgiven yourself?"

Stephanie snorted. "Forgive myself? My mistakes are too high to even dent. I try to forget about everything I did before God got through to me, but forgive? No."

"God forgave you. Shouldn't you do the same?"

"I'll add it to my to-do list."

Bea laughed. "Be sure to check it off when you get to it."

"I don't know what I would do without you. Thank you for listening and not judging. I don't blame you if—"

"Stop right there. I love you. End of story."

"I don't deserve—"

Bea made a tut-tut noise. "End of story."

"And the rooster says, 'cock-a-doodle-doo,' and the ducky says, 'quack quack quack,' and the piggy says, 'oink oink oink'…"

She didn't have time for this. Stephanie stabbed the calculator buttons Thursday night, but the sum flashing back at her didn't make sense. Her pencil rolled off the stack of papers to the floor. She had to finish this report. If only she could have some peace, but there wasn't a chance of that happening.

What time was it anyway? Tom would be there soon, which meant she'd have to entertain him. Tonight was their first meeting since the pumpkin patch last weekend, and Macy hadn't quite warmed up to him then. Stephanie had a feeling they were in for an awkward hour, an hour she'd have to bring her A game to in order to get the two of them used to each other. Was a headache coming on? Yes. Yes, it was.

"...and the dalmatian says, 'woofy woofy,' and the goosey says, 'honk honk'..." The song grew louder as Macy added more words and ran back and forth from the couch to the rocking chair, crashing into the cushions with each new verse.

"Macy!" Stephanie whirled in her chair. "Keep it down. You know the rule about homework. I have a lot to do, and I need it to be quiet."

"Sorry, Mommy." Her joy disappeared as she hugged the floppy stuffed bunny Tom gave her.

Stephanie's stomach plummeted. She'd over-reacted again. The poor kid had no one to play with, was entertaining herself by singing, and all Stephanie could do was yell. She would never be up for a mother-of-the-year award. Torn between continuing the assignment and playing with Macy for a few minutes, she closed her eyes instead.

Lord, I'm having a hard time here. Macy is bored and lonely. And driving me nuts. I don't want to yell, but this report is important. I'm tired of feeling so guilty. Help?

"And the snakey says, 'slither slither slither,' and the crocodile says..." Macy sang loudly.

Stephanie's temple throbbed, but she bit back another holler. She sighed and tried to focus on the columns. The intercom buzzed.

Six-thirty already? She smoothed her wine-colored sweater over her black pants—she hadn't bothered changing after work and school—and hoped her makeup had stayed put from this morning. Why couldn't she have gotten more of the report finished during her lunch break?

"Hi, Tom." Stephanie ushered him inside, casting a glance at the papers on the table to her left. "Come on in."

His tall body dwarfed the couch. Macy had disappeared, leaving a trail of stuffed animals in her wake. The girl refused to play alone in her room, but now that Tom had arrived, her room had become a welcome destination? Figured.

"I'll get Macy," she said. "Just a minute."

She strode down the hallway and opened Macy's door. "Tom's here."

Macy sat on the floor with two baby dolls. She stuck a fake bottle near one's mouth.

"Did you hear me?" Stephanie waited in the doorway. "It's time to come out to the living room."

Glaring, Macy swiped one of the dolls up. Then she trudged into the hallway. When she reached the living room, she didn't say a word. Just sat cross-legged on the floor and pretended to feed her baby.

"Aren't you going to say hello?" Stephanie motioned for Macy to greet Tom.

"Hello." She didn't glance up.

Stephanie opened her mouth to reprimand her, but Tom leaned forward, elbows on his spread knees, and pointed to the doll. "What's your little boy's name?"

Macy jerked to attention. "This is a girl. A baby girl."

"Nah, it's a boy. Anybody can see it."

Macy's scowl could have dimmed the entire building. "She's a girl. It's Emily."

Tom scratched his chin, a confused look on his face. "Are you sure about that? It looks exactly like my brother Sam when he was a baby."

Macy stared at Tom, then at the doll.

"In fact, I'd say the baby's real name is Sam."

"It is not! It's Emily." She cradled Emily tightly against her sling. "And she's a girl."

Stephanie stood between the living room and dining area. Should she step in? Say something? This meeting was starting out as disastrously as the last one had.

"Bring it over." Tom crooked two fingers at the doll. "I need to see this for myself."

Macy uncurled her legs, marched to him and thrust Emily into his hands. "See? She's a girl. She's wearing a pink dress. Boys don't wear dresses."

He held the doll away from him and squinted at it. Then he brought it closer. "Well, I'll be. This *is* a girl. How could I have thought it was a boy? Doesn't even look like my brother now I'm up close, except Sam does wear a pink shirt on occasion. Must be where I went wrong."

Macy put her hand over her mouth and giggled. "Do you want to see my other baby? Briana?"

"Of course I do. Why wouldn't I? Wait, is this Briana one of those babies that goes to the bathroom?"

"No-o." She shifted her weight to one hip and put her free hand on her waist. "My babies are good babies."

"I hope you're right, cuz I don't like stinky diapers."

Macy hopped up and down, clapping. "I think she has a stinky diaper."

"Then leave her in the other room." He stretched his hands out in a stopping motion. His eyes shimmered, teased. Macy raced out of there with wicked glee.

"You handle her well." Stephanie hitched her chin toward him.

His mischievous side disappeared, leaving questions and uncertainty in its place. "I don't know."

"I'm sorry she's been so—" She kept her voice soft, but Macy tore back into the room with a baby in one hand and a play diaper tucked into her sling. Her eyes sparkled above flushed cheeks. Excitement sizzled in the air.

"Yep, Tom, Briana has a dirty diaper!" She held the doll right up to his face.

His expression transformed to mock horror. "A dirty diaper? Yuck." He held his nose between his fingers and waved with his other hand.

"She's really stinky." Macy pushed the baby to him.

"Well, go change her diaper!"

"No!" she squealed. "You do it!"

He fanned himself. "I can't. I would melt."

Stephanie slipped away and sat at the table, unexpected tears pressing against the backs of her eyes. She'd never guessed this side of Tom existed, had never seen him interact with a child. He'd broken through Macy's bad attitude with teasing—hadn't had to yell. She bowed her head, blinking back the emotion. If she had known he could be such a caring dad, would she have done things differently?

"You're doing it wrong, Tom." Macy's haughty tone made it clear she was thrilled to have the upper hand. "The diaper doesn't go there!"

Stephanie jerked her head up and looked over her shoulder. Tom wrestled a diaper around the baby's shoulders. She stifled a laugh. Macy lunged for the diaper. "No, no, no! It's not a vest, silly!"

"Macy," he said in a deep, low voice. "I think you're going to have to teach me about this baby stuff. I don't have a clue what I'm doing."

Stephanie craned her neck to see Macy's reaction. She heaved the baby out of his hands and set it on the couch. "It's easy. Don't worry. You'll get it." She laid the diaper out and put Briana on it. "Then this part goes up here, and this sticker thingy goes over here, and—"

"Hold up." Tom lifted his nose and pretended to sniff. "Do you smell that?"

Macy's eyes grew round, anticipation dancing within. "No."

"You don't smell it?" He sounded incredulous. Stephanie suppressed a laugh, certain where this was going.

"I don't smell anything 'cept Mama's spicy candle."

He pointed to the doll. "The baby went potty again. It smells real bad."

Macy's forehead furrowed; then she grinned. "She did! She stinks! You change her." She tossed poor Briana into the air toward Tom.

"No way!" He dodged the doll. "*You* change her."

Stephanie frowned. They didn't need her. All it took was a couple of baby dolls and pretend dirty diapers and he'd wrapped her daughter—their daughter—around his finger. If she had known…

No. No more regrets. Besides, what he was doing was the easy part. Time would tell if she could trust him to see this relationship through. Macy wasn't a toy to pick up and set down at will. If Tom wanted to be her father, he'd have to commit to Macy forever, not just show up for a few months and fade away, busy with his own life.

But Stephanie had to admit, she liked seeing this side of him, loved the way he made Macy laugh.

And—she smiled—since they obviously didn't need her, she was going to work on her report.

Tom opened an orange Powerade, wiped the sweat off his forehead with a towel and swallowed a gulp on his way to his bedroom Friday night. Right after work he'd pounded out five miles on the treadmill, then tried out his new stationary bike. With winter almost here, his days of cycling outside were numbered. Of course, nothing beat the real thing, but he could adjust the speed and incline to mimic hills—a good enough substitute. The one piece of the triathlon puzzle he still worried about was the swimming portion. He could handle himself in a pool, but his form wasn't good enough to excel in the 2.4-mile open-water swim.

After a quick shower, he changed into sweatpants and a faded Detroit Tigers tee and fell onto the couch. Bryan must have come home while Tom was in the shower, because he stood behind the open fridge door, scanning the contents. "Didn't you go to the store?"

Tom looked up from flipping through channels. "Yeah, why?"

"There's nothing in here." Bryan slammed it shut. "I'm ordering a pizza."

"What are you talking about?" Tom breezed into the kitchen and opened the fridge. "There's tons of food in here. If you'll give me half an hour, I'll grill us some chicken breasts. There's broccoli and brown rice to go with it."

In black pants, pin-striped shirt and tie, Bryan leaned against the counter and glowered. "You've got to be kidding me. We had chicken four times last week. Just hearing the word *broccoli* makes me hurl. See that? I threw up a little. I'm getting a pizza."

Tom blocked his path, which was easy to do in the small kitchen. The out-of-date oak cabinets, beige Formica counters and boring cream vinyl floors looked tired. His eating and exercising habits weren't the only areas in his life needing an overhaul. They should update the bungalow. "What's wrong with eating healthier?"

"You might be living the dream, but I'm a normal person. It's Friday. I want to live in the real world. A world where we eat hot wings and nachos. Pizza. Brownies." Bryan brushed past him, loosening his tie in the process. "How long until I get my brother back?"

"About nine months." Nine months, two weeks and three days to be exact. "Why don't you work out with me? I signed up for private swimming lessons at the Y. We can swim laps."

Bryan glared, unbuttoning his collar, cell phone in his other hand. "You're killing me."

"What's wrong with swimming?"

"I'm not spending every waking free hour working out. No way. Hey, I give you credit, man, but it's not for me."

"You'll change your mind."

Bryan's disgusted look said it all.

Tom bit back a laugh. He'd better change the subject before his brother punched him. "What do you think about the new truck models? We've almost cleared out last year's inventory. Only have six left. What about you?"

Bryan brightened. "Yeah, sales are great right now." He managed the two other auto dealerships. Their grandfather had started Sheffield Auto on a vacant lot surrounded by cornfields about four miles from town. Within ten years, Granddad had added another dealership, eventually owning and running five total in two counties. Dad took over the operation in the mid-1980s. They had to shut one location down during the last recession, but

Tom and Bryan owned and operated the remaining four. Sam was CEO of the company, and Dad and their sisters had a share in the overall profits. "I'm thinking about buying a new four-by-four."

"Already? Don't tell me you're tired of the silver monster out front." Bryan switched out vehicles the way their little sister Libby changed clothes—frequently.

Bryan shrugged, held up a finger and pressed buttons on the phone. "Give me a minute. I'm ordering."

Tom rolled his eyes but waited for Bryan to order a double-meat pizza.

"You were saying?" A gleam lit Bryan's eye.

"You're bored."

"What?" Bryan's chest swelled. "I'm not bored. Just because your life shifted into hyperdrive doesn't mean mine's boring." He tossed his tie onto the table and dropped to the couch. "How did it go last night anyway? You guys going to tell her soon?"

"Not yet." Tom sprawled out on the recliner. "I've only seen Macy twice. She barely knows me."

"So it didn't go well?" Bryan clicked through the channels, stopping at ESPN.

"I didn't say that. Last night was good. She's less standoffish, you know, warming up."

"How warm does she need to be? It doesn't

change the fact she's your kid. She doesn't have to like you. I'm surprised you let Stephanie have her way on this. I hope she isn't trying to weasel her way out of letting you see Macy."

"Why would she do that?"

"It's the old 'Well, Macy doesn't feel comfortable with you, so I'd better keep her and never let you see her. It's for her best interests' bit. Why is Stephanie keeping it a big secret? I mean… Wait—" Bryan twisted to stare at him. "It's a trick. A trick to either get you back or get you off her back. I wouldn't put it past her."

Tom ground his teeth together. "It's not a trick. Do you really think I'm stupid enough to get involved with her again? I've been down that road, brother, and we both know how it turned out."

"Then why is she so insistent you spend all this time together?"

"We've spent three hours together."

Bryan's stare probed.

His brother didn't get it. If their positions were switched, he'd probably say the same thing. And Bryan knew divorce firsthand. His marriage had made it barely a year.

"Hey, man," Tom said. "I get what you're saying, but it's not like that. You'll understand when you see Macy. She's young. Used to being with her mom all the time. This is all new for her, too."

Bryan leveled a look full of disbelief at him. "With her mom *all* the time? I doubt it."

Everything Bryan said had a grain of truth to it. "We'll tell Macy when the time is right. I don't care what Stephanie's motives are. All that matters to me now is being there for my daughter."

They listened to the college football predictions, but Tom couldn't concentrate. His brother lacked tact, but he also brought up good points. What he'd told Bryan was true—he had no intention of falling for Stephanie again.

But...what if this *was* a ploy to keep him from claiming Macy?

He let his eyes close and took a deep breath. The day at the pumpkin patch Stephanie had been careful to keep Macy between them. Yesterday, she'd made sure Macy came out to the living room to spend time with him—and she'd left them alone to work on her report. If she was trying to keep him from developing a relationship with Macy, she had a funny way of showing it.

As far as wanting him back, Tom doubted she'd ever wanted him in the first place.

She'd been attracted to him. He didn't doubt that. He'd wooed her, proposed. The light in her eyes had told him she was interested, but after they were married...he didn't know. Maybe she had loved him, but he hadn't paid attention.

Bryan had one thing right, though. They

couldn't play "let's pretend" forever. Next time he saw Stephanie, Tom would broach the subject of when they should tell Macy the truth.

Chapter Five

"Stay here." Stephanie tightened her grip on Macy's hand as they waited in line a week later. From the looks of it, every kid in the city had come to Chuck E. Cheese's tonight. A hint of aftershave drifted to her. She snuck a peek at Tom. His wide shoulders filled out his light blue button-down shirt rolled up at the sleeves, and his jeans fit him perfectly. Not that she'd noticed.

The line inched forward, and Macy tugged on Stephanie's hand. The doctor had checked Macy's wrist yesterday and declared her healed enough to get rid of the sling. "Come on, Mommy."

"Wait." She glanced at Tom. "Are you sure about this?"

"Yeah, why? I hear this is the place to have fun. Isn't that right, Macy?"

"Yeah!"

Have fun…or misplace a child. How could anyone keep track of a kid in this chaos?

They reached the front of the line. Tom ordered a large pizza, drinks and tokens, and he pulled out his wallet. Stephanie set her hand on his. "Let me."

He shook his head, presenting his credit card to the kid behind the counter. "I've got it. Why don't you find us a table?"

"And leave you to carry everything?" She reached for the tray the clerk passed to them.

"Seriously, Steph?" He grabbed it before she could react. His use of her nickname stunned her into silence. She hadn't been called Steph since they were married. "I can handle a tray with three empty cups."

"I know, but—"

"Macy, did your mom forget I'm working out?" He winked, pretending to flex his biceps.

"No-o, silly. She remembers." Her pigtails bounced. "Let's go play!"

Yes, she remembered. The fact was, Stephanie remembered everything about him. The first time she saw him her pulse had practically jolted out of her skin. The first words he'd said to her— "Nice shirt"—with an amused grin at the tailgating party they'd both attended. He had a way of setting her at ease. She'd tucked it all in her heart—the proposal, the dazzling diamond ring, the love in his gaze when he met her at the end of the aisle. The hatred he'd poured out during their final fight.

She remembered it all.

"We have to find a table first." Stephanie led Macy to the dining area.

"How about here?" Macy's face glowed. Stephanie sidestepped a trio of young boys racing to the arcade games.

"Well…" Stephanie cleared her thoughts to focus on now. "How many seats do we need?"

"Three."

"And how many does this have?"

Macy pointed her finger as she counted. "Six."

"It's probably a good idea to get a smaller table so a big family will have someplace to sit."

Macy scanned the empty tables. "I see one. Over there." She tore free from Stephanie's grasp and ran toward the windows.

"Macy, wait." Stephanie barely heard her own voice over the din. She wove through families and caught up as Macy slid into a booth.

"See? This fits us." Macy spread her arms wide and grinned.

"Yes, it does, but don't run off like that again. See how many kids are here? I don't want to lose you, so stay close."

Tom set the tray on the table and handed them

each a soda. "What do you say, Macy? Should we wait for the pizza or play some games first?"

"Games!"

"Atta girl." He turned to Stephanie. "Want to come?"

"No." She shook her head. "You two go on. I'll wait here for the pizza."

She stood to let Macy out of the booth and bit her lip at the picture they presented—Tom, tall and strong, holding Macy's tiny hand as she skipped down the aisle, every now and then staring up at him in adoration. It hadn't taken long for her little girl to become infatuated.

Oh, Macy. Just like your mama.

She leaned back, allowed herself a few moments of peace. Well, as peaceful as a Chuck E. Cheese's on a Friday night in late October could be. A young girl with two blond braids ran by. Dance music from the giant television screen filled in any gaps. A piercing temper tantrum added to the mayhem, but for the first time in months, Stephanie relaxed. Really relaxed. Didn't think. Just sat there. Content.

To not have to worry about Macy right now—to not have to make sure she was entertained—to simply rest and breathe? What a gift.

Stephanie had gone out to lunch with Bea again today. Wise and kind, Bea helped Stephanie more than she knew. But their conversation had brought questions up, too. Questions Stephanie wasn't prepared to answer.

Like did she trust Tom with Macy? How would she feel when the two of them went off alone? Was she ready to give up holidays and weekends with her daughter when he filed for custody? And how could she be sure he wasn't going to punish her for lying to him? Stephanie craned her neck to locate them. She rose slightly, not seeing much beyond the Skee-Ball machines and the network of play tubes reaching to the ceiling. Chuck E. Cheese himself strutted by, shaking hands with every kid who would let him.

Where were they?

No need to be nervous. Tom had Macy. They were probably around the corner where more games lurked. Nothing to worry about.

A waiter chose that moment to set the pizza and paper plates on the table. She lowered back into her seat but continued scanning the floor, trying to see either Macy or Tom. Or both.

"Can I get you anything else, miss?" the waiter asked.

"No, thanks." The mozzarella cheese and Italian spices made her stomach growl, but she pressed her hand against her abdomen and turned in her seat, desperate to spot Macy.

"Ah, dinner has arrived." Tom's masculine

voice startled her, and she jerked back, her palm on her chest.

"Let me in, Mama." Macy poked her. Stephanie stepped out to let her settle into the corner. Tom served them each a slice, and Macy wasted no time tearing into it. Cheese stretched from her mouth to the pizza. "I won tickets!"

"You did?" Stephanie handed her a napkin. "How many?"

She shrugged, concentrating on chewing. Then she sipped her drink. "Lots."

Tom held up several folded rows of gray tickets. "After we eat, we can win more." He shook the plastic cup holding the tokens. "Then you can pick out your prizes."

"This is the best place ever!" She dropped her pizza and clapped her hands, bouncing in her seat.

"Yes, yes," Stephanie said. "It's a wonderland. But first you have to eat."

Macy nodded, already taking another bite. Her pleasure brought Stephanie mixed feelings. She wanted Macy to be excited, but she didn't want her getting used to this kind of extravagance. On a tight budget, Stephanie couldn't afford pizzas out and games and all the fun Tom promised.

"Is something wrong?" Tom slid two slices of pizza onto his plate.

She couldn't compete with this. Not now, at

least. Maybe in a few years when she had a better-paying job. "No, nothing's wrong. It's been a grueling week." She picked at her pizza. "Tell me more about this IRONMAN thing."

He lifted his finger until he finished chewing. "It's my first competition. August. Right now I'm getting in shape. By the end of January, I'll begin my serious workouts."

"What exactly is involved?"

Macy paid no attention to them as she ate and watched the other kids.

"I'm building up how many miles I run and bike. I joined the Y here, too, since Lake Endwell doesn't have any indoor pools. The race starts with a 2.4-mile swim in open water. Then I hop on a bike for 112 miles. Finally, I run 26.2 miles. My goal is to finish under twelve hours."

"Why twelve hours?"

"The average time is twelve and a half—I'm going to beat that."

"Impressive." She leaned forward, resting her chin on her hand. "I'm sure it isn't easy with your work schedule."

A pang of hurt crossed his face, but he nodded. "It isn't, but it's important to me."

She dropped her gaze to the table and crumpled a napkin. "I know how exhausting work is, how much it takes out of you. And now that I'm in school full-time, too, well, I understand sacrificing to go after a dream."

His eyes reminded her of Lake Endwell on a clear summer day. Enticing.

"So you want to be an accountant?"

"I know, I know, hard to believe, right?" She let out an embarrassed laugh. Her grades had never been great, but now she earned more As than Bs, and she was proud of them.

"Not so hard to believe." He stretched his arm across the back of the booth. "Why accounting?"

"Good pay, flexible hours."

He didn't respond, but a thoughtful expression softened his features. He finished eating his slice, and Stephanie took another bite of hers, but her appetite hadn't been good all week. Too many changes. Too many things to think about. The biggest one sat across from her.

He still mesmerized her.

She could not think that way. Not again. Never again.

"I'm ready to win more tickets." Macy wiped her hands over her empty plate and grinned. "Are you coming, Mommy?"

"I'm going to sit here and rest while you and Tom win them, okay?"

"Okay." She pouted a second, but when Stephanie let her out of the booth, she perked right up. "Come on—let's go to the light-up game!"

"Your wish is my command, Princess Macy."

Stephanie groaned. First Chuck E. Cheese's. Now a princess? Macy would be impossible to live with after tonight.

Later that night, Tom followed Stephanie into her apartment, inhaling the cinnamon scent he'd come to enjoy. Macy had fallen asleep in his truck, so he carried her inside and laid her on her bed, which was covered with a pink-and-purple-polka-dotted comforter. An old chest of drawers with chipped white paint stood opposite. Pink curtains hung from the windows, and stuffed animals were stashed in an inexpensive laundry basket. Girlie. He smiled.

He kissed Macy's forehead, slipped her small shoes off her feet and covered her with the comforter, then joined Stephanie in the living room.

"Will she be okay? Does she need pajamas or anything?" He lowered himself onto the couch, but his leg refused to stay still. Even when he pushed it down with his hand, his knee bounced. What he had to say stuck in his throat.

"I don't want to wake her. She'll be fine." She flopped in the rocking chair, her slim frame slouching as she ran a finger across her forehead. "Thanks for tonight."

"She had a good time," he said, trying not to gape at how beautiful she looked. "I didn't realize it would take fifteen minutes for her to pick out her prizes, though."

Stephanie laughed. "She's never been there. I don't buy her many toys, so when she gets them, it's a big deal."

As good an opening as he was going to get. "It's time to change that."

"She'll live without a mountain of toys."

"That's not what I meant. I'm her dad. I want to provide for her. When are we going to tell her the truth? Make this official?"

Her smile slid off her face as she straightened, blinked twice. "What are you going to do?"

"I'm not doing anything," he said quickly. "We agreed to let Macy get used to me before telling her. Well, I think she's about ready."

"That's it?" She bit her lower lip. "You just want to tell her?"

"Well, no. Of course not." He rose, massaging the back of his neck. "I want more. You know I want to be her father. I am her father."

The startled look on her face didn't reassure him.

"Are you asking for custody?" she asked quietly.

He began to pace. "Not full custody if that's what you mean. But, yeah, I want to share her, and I don't want a visit now and then when it's convenient for you. I want joint custody."

"Joint custody. I see."

"I'm not being unreasonable. I'll pay child support—in fact, I want to pay it." He held out a hand, trying not to offend her. "But I am pursuing this. I've already talked to my lawyer. Is my name on the birth certificate?"

Her face paled. "Yes."

"Good, it will simplify things. I'll sign an acknowledgment of paternity. You and I can work out a schedule for me to have Macy." He roamed back and forth between the couch and television. All the problems and details he'd dug up swam around, fighting for attention. "I think we'll have to talk to a friend of the court, get a judge's signature, and we should be all set."

"Signatures. Friend of the…" She shook her head. "Tom?"

"Hmm?"

"I've got to know—please don't take this the wrong way—will you be there for her, really be there for her?"

He slowly spun and stared at her.

She wrung her hands. "It's not that I don't want you to share custody—you just found out and you're excited, I get it—but three years from now will you still want…" She spread her hands out and lifted her shoulders.

"Yes, Stephanie," he ground out. "I will still want my daughter. Do you have any idea what it's been like for me to know I've had a little girl all this time but had no clue she existed? You sit there and have the nerve to ask me if I'll be there for her, like she's a toy I'll outgrow." He averted his gaze. "I don't think you know me at all. But maybe I shouldn't be surprised. We were married, we lived together and you didn't know me then, either."

"I knew you," she murmured. "I know you. And this is not about you or me or our marriage. It's about Macy. I'm the one who's taken care of her 24/7 since the second she was born."

"And why is that, Stephanie?" A burning sensation rose in his chest. Was she hinting he was to blame? A hard coating spread over his heart.

"We've been through this." She stood, throwing her hands up. "Can you honestly say you wouldn't have demanded we stay together for her sake? You would have resented me. Resented her. I'm fierce for her, Tom. I'll do anything to protect her."

He bit back his reply and considered her words. Would he have resented a child back then? Demanded they stay together? He wouldn't have served the divorce papers. Stephanie had him there. But as far as the other...

She moved next to him and touched his forearm. He flinched.

"Maybe I want to protect her, too." He held

himself rigid. "Maybe I don't like the thought of her living in a run-down apartment in a not-so-safe neighborhood. Maybe I'm not crazy about the fact she spends all day in a day care center while you work. Maybe I'd like for her to know my family—the aunts and uncles who will adore her. It's not fair to them or to her to miss out on each other."

She swallowed. "What are you suggesting? You *are* going to ask for full custody, aren't you?"

"Is that what this is about?" Some of the fight left him. "You're afraid I'm going to take her away from you? I'd never do that, Stephanie. I'm not the monster you think I am."

"I've never thought you were a monster, Tom." She angled away from him. "If anyone was a monster, it was me. I…I wish I had done things differently."

His fury dissipated as quickly as it had come on. Her defeated stance, the regret in her eyes, made him want to touch her, to tell her it was all right. But he didn't.

"I don't know what I'd do without her." Conviction and fear colored her words. "I've made too many mistakes. How many times have I gone back in my mind and been the wife you needed?"

Understanding flashed then—she didn't blame him for their failed marriage. She blamed herself. *Forgive her, Tom.*

What? Where had that thought come from? He balled his fists down by his sides.

Forgive her.

Clenching his jaw, he gave his head a slight shake. He couldn't. Not yet.

You can.

His fists uncurled. Jaw loosened. And he studied the wounded woman standing so close to him. Close enough to run his hand down her hair, comfort her if he chose to.

He wanted to.

Gently, he touched her hair. So silky.

"We both made mistakes. I just want to spend time with her, too."

She inhaled sharply, her expression questioning before she broke into a smile. "I'm glad. I'm glad you want to spend time with her."

"What gave you the idea I wouldn't?" Her floral perfume soothed him as much as her words did.

She averted her eyes. "I'm a product of divorce, Tom. I've been through it."

"But you spent all kinds of time with your dad."

"Yeah. I did. And where was my mom?"

He thought back. Stephanie's mom hadn't been in the picture except for a brief appearance at their wedding. She rarely talked about her. "You lived with your mom through high school."

"No, I didn't." She retreated to the chair. "I lived with her and my stepfather of the month until I turned twelve. Then I moved in with Dad."

"What happened?" He resumed his position on the couch. Leaning forward, he rested his elbows on his knees, his clasped hands dangling between.

"Husband number three. He lived in Chicago, and Mom planned on moving there. We all decided it would be best if I didn't have to change schools, so I went with Dad."

"But you still talked to her? Saw her?" He fit the puzzle together as best he could, but he was missing a dozen pieces.

"Sure. Now and then. Honestly, she and I weren't very close when we lived together. She cycled through being depressed, dating, in the honeymoon phase or powering through a divorce. I couldn't keep up. But she loved me in her own way."

Explained a lot. He cracked his knuckles, wanting to protect her from the pain. Her delicate face radiated youthful vitality, but it was shadowed by the hard edges of experience.

She flicked her wrist. "Mom can be fun and generous and loving—as loving as anyone I know. I wanted too much from her."

"Too much? She's your mother. She owed you that."

Stephanie shook her head. "No. Nobody owes me anything. Anyway, Macy is blessed to have you, and you have every right to see her. We'll work out an arrangement."

"Thank you." The glimpse of her childhood pain made his stomach tighten. Her worries about Macy made more sense. He cleared his throat. "I was thinking we could figure out a schedule in the next couple of weeks, get the legal things rolling and tell Macy around Thanksgiving."

"Thanksgiving?"

"My family is dying to meet her." He couldn't wait to introduce her to them all. "Is that a problem?"

"No, no. But my dad is coming for Thanksgiving."

"So? Bring him."

"What? I'm confused." She brushed fuzz off the sleeve of her sweater. "You want me there, too?"

"Well, yeah. Why not? You know everyone. It would be pretty intimidating for Macy to meet all the Sheffields if you're not there. But we have to tell her who I am first. I want to make it special."

"This is all happening so fast." She crossed the room and set her fingers on the edge of the table.

"Not for me." He followed her, lured by her honesty. "It's not happening fast enough. I've got lost time to make up for."

"I know. We'll work out an agreement between now and then." She wrapped her arms around her body. "I'm a little nervous."

"Did you think I'd pretend to be an old friend forever?"

"No. It's just…well, you've seen the fun parts of being a parent. It's not all princesses, stuffed animals and pizzas. It's disciplining and paying attention when you have other things to do."

"I get that, Steph. I'm not an idiot." He stepped away from her at the tension her words produced.

"I didn't mean that the way it came out. You have integrity—always have. I envied you your morals, you know, when we were married. I wanted your attention… I'm sorry for what I put you through." She lifted her chin, her eyes shimmering. "It'll be good for Macy to have a father. To have you as a dad."

"Hey," he said, his throat tight. "I was at fault, too. I…" Dare he say this to her? Admit it? Out loud? "I wasn't a good husband. I didn't pay attention to you. Assumed your world should revolve around me. I took you for granted, and I'm sorry. We were both too young."

A sad smile flitted over her lips. "You can say that again."

Chapter Six

Monday afternoon, Stephanie sat in her new car, a white four-door Ford with only three patches of rust. With fifteen minutes before class started, this was one place she could have a private phone conversation. "Tom wants joint custody."

"You know how I feel about it." Dad's steady tone calmed her nerves. While he'd accepted her decision not to tell Tom, he'd never agreed with it. "It's about time he knew. It will be good for them. And for you."

"No offense, Dad, but how could it be good for me?" She grabbed her coupon envelope and sorted them by expiration date. After she picked up Macy from day care, she had to shop for a few groceries. Then she had a spreadsheet to create.

"You can let go of the guilt. Besides, when was the last time you had a break?" Two seconds passed. "I'll tell you. Last year. When you lived with me. I don't like that you and Macy are alone. You'll run yourself ragged. Why don't you finish your degree here? I have plenty of room."

She crumpled an expired cereal coupon. "I'm so close to finishing, Dad. It won't be long—less than a year—and we'll be down there. Besides, I'd lose my scholarship if I leave. I don't want to pay for tuition if I don't have to."

"Yeah, yeah, I told you I'd pay it," he said. "You're still coming for Christmas, though, right?"

"Of course. But our Thanksgiving plans have changed. Tom and I are telling Macy before Thanksgiving. He wants to introduce her to his family then."

"And you're going to just let my granddaughter get thrust into his overbearing family on her own?"

She sighed. "No. Tom wants me there. He invited you, too."

Silence stretched. "He wants you there, huh? I don't like it."

"Why not? You're the one who always told me what a mistake I was making not telling him."

"Yeah, but I didn't think— Never mind."

"It's to make Macy feel comfortable. Why, what are you trying to say?" She tossed the coupon pack on the passenger seat and stared out the windshield. The branches had lost their leaves and left dark outlines against the not-quite-white sky. She shivered. Dreary.

"He thinks you come with the package."

"It's not like that, Dad."

"Then what is it? Revenge?"

If Dad had asked her this the day Tom found out, she might have considered it. But not now. "Point taken, but I don't think so. We've been talking. It brought up painful parts of the past. I think we've both matured."

He grunted. "He sees you've become a beautiful woman with a special little girl. A ready-made family. His family. Be careful. You don't want to end up right where you started."

She closed her eyes. Tom's oh-so-gentle touch to her hair came to mind. The tenderness he showed to Macy. His big, open smile. His parting words last night—ones she never expected to hear. Ones she'd desperately needed.

"We're not getting back together," she said.

"Are you sure about that?"

Was she? "Yeah, I'm sure. We're compromising for Macy's sake, but what's done is done. He'll never forgive me."

"What if he did?"

She let it sit there, tried it on. And she saw herself the way she'd been before the divorce. Scared. Insecure. "I have goals in life, Dad, and I'm not getting involved with anyone until I see them through. I'm too busy anyway. I barely have time to study now. I have my own plans, and I'm not giving them up."

"Good. Stay strong. I believe in you."

"Thanks." They chatted a few more minutes before hanging up.

Dad had been the one constant in her life since she was a child. He'd never missed a weekend after her parents split when she was six. While Mom busied herself planning her weddings, Dad drove Stephanie to dance classes. When Mom kept her up late moaning about men and nursing a bottle of wine, Dad confronted Mom about Stephanie having a normal bedtime.

He'd provided for her. Bought her school supplies, made sure she had flute lessons and rides to volleyball practices. She appreciated all of it, even though they'd struggled to communicate when she was in high school. They always got along fine—she just had a hard time confiding in him about friends or grades or her other problems. Whenever she'd tried, he would get nervous and mumble Mr. Fix-It advice that didn't make much sense. Still, she loved him. And as she grew older, their relationship had grown deeper.

Grabbing her books and purse, she locked the car and walked toward the school building. Cold air nipped at her face. She tucked her chin and forced her legs to move faster.

Dad worried she was getting back together with Tom. How had he put it? Back to where she started.

Dad was wrong.

Marriage to Tom reminded her of life with Mom. Stephanie had been in the backseat for both relationships. She could handle a lot of things, but being invisible wasn't one of them.

An icy blast whipped her hair. Brr...like it or not, winter had arrived.

Miami. Sun. Dad. A few months before they'd be together again. The three of them. The way it used to be.

But what about Tom?

He didn't know about Florida. She'd have to tell him. And when he tried to talk her out of it? She'd deal with it later.

"Seven more laps. Finish strong."

Tom circled one arm over the other in the lap pool at the YMCA Tuesday night. His first lesson with Sean had been Saturday morning. The strokes weren't difficult, but getting his form correct proved challenging. He surged through the water and concentrated on his breathing.

Alive.

He felt alive challenging his body.

The water rushed over his skin, and his muscles stretched as he propelled forward. Nothing like pushing his body to the limit. In control.

He finished the laps and hoisted up to sit on the edge of the pool. "How did I look?"

"Better." Sean wrote something on a clipboard. "The first twenty laps had breaks in your form, but the last ten were almost there."

Good. Improvement.

"Come in tomorrow night, and I'll give you a new workout."

Tom got to his feet and grabbed his towel. Lined with windows, the pool area displayed a tranquil view of several pines. Christmas trees. He wiped his body down and made his way to the locker room.

He'd talked to Stephanie earlier. They were meeting Thursday during her lunch hour to discuss a visitation schedule. Adding swim times to his busy day complicated things. He divided time equally between his two dealerships. He used to stay late each night catching up on paperwork, but he couldn't fit in a full training session when he worked overtime. Today he'd eaten lunch at his desk to deal with the orders, statements and never-ending emails. When would he get caught up?

If Stephanie agreed to let him have Macy for a few hours two nights a week, he'd have to schedule his swimming around it. The weekends made him nervous, too. Saturdays were his big workout day, the day he planned on adding hours each week to all three events—running, bicycling and swimming. How could he do that and watch Macy? And what about end-of-the-month quotas at work?

After lifting the latch on his locker, he opened it and jerked out his clothes. He'd figure it out. How many dads dealt with this every day? Seeing his kid, working and training couldn't be that hard.

Still…he'd better come up with a plan before his meeting with Stephanie.

He ran the towel over his head. What about overnight visits? He and Bryan had converted the basement to a gym this summer. Where would Macy sleep?

Pulling on his shirt, he ticked through the options. He wasn't making her sleep on their beat-up leather couch. Who knew what odors and crumbs lurked inside? He wanted Macy to have her own spot, a pretty room of her own where she could have toys and a bed, and she'd be comfortable.

But where?

He grimaced, slammed the locker shut and finished dressing.

Maybe it was time to buy his own place.

"I've never eaten here before." Stephanie craned her neck to take in the dark, elegant restaurant. Midnight blue walls stood out against gleaming dark hardwood floors. Modern lighting brought a glow to the square black tables, and a fireplace to the side added coziness. She set her purse on the empty chair. "Remember, I have to be back to work in one hour."

"I know. Don't worry." Tom's smile reached his eyes—be still her heart—and he opened a menu. "This place is pretty good about getting you in and out."

She hoped so. The dentist she worked for didn't put up with tardiness, and her job meant too much for her to jeopardize. A lunch date—scratch that, not date, *meeting*—made the most sense, though. She didn't want to hire a babysitter for Macy after work. Plus, she had to study for a test later. There were never enough hours in the day.

"What's good here?" She picked up her menu. Her stomach had been a war zone since last night. Agreeing on a visitation schedule—a scary, scary thing. What if he wanted Macy when it wasn't convenient for Stephanie? And how would this affect her and Macy's relationship? She'd been number one in their daughter's life. She didn't want to become number two.

"You'd probably like the angel-hair pasta." The menu hid his face. "The lemon butter sauce is light."

Her breath caught. He remembered. She loved

lemon butter sauce. Why did something insignificant matter so much right now?

A waiter brought two waters and wrote their orders on a narrow pad of paper. She inhaled. Prepared herself. Tom opened a briefcase.

"I don't know how this is usually done," he said. "But I did an online search and found out what kind of schedules other people have come up with."

Stephanie traced the rim of her water glass. Until this moment, her plan to move to Florida next year had seemed possible. But—she glanced at Tom, his eyebrows drawn together as he opened a folder and took out papers—she'd been lying to herself.

He handed her a single sheet of paper with some sort of chart on it. She scanned it and met his gaze over the drinks. The schedule in front of her might work for next-door neighbors. Who didn't have jobs. The time was divided almost equally. Her mind reeled with the challenges it involved. She held it up. "I don't know about this."

"It's a sample. I don't think you and I could manage anything like that being thirty minutes away from each other. So I thought about it and wrote down what I hoped for. Here—take a look." He slid her another paper. She read it over and heaved a sigh. *Much better.*

"So you want two evenings a week and every other weekend with her until she's in school full-time?"

He nodded, a curtain of uncertainty dimming his expression. "I might have a problem, though, in the summer. Would you be willing to adjust the schedule for about six weeks before the race? I'll have to go all out with my training then, and I might not be able to swing every other weekend."

"That won't be a problem." The more time she had with Macy, the better.

His lips curved up. Was relief brightening his face? "We'll have to consider what's best for her. She'll be in school next year, which is a big commitment. I want to make sure she's not over-booked."

Next year... Stephanie averted her gaze. She might be living in Florida. With Dad. And Macy.

"Tom," she said, biting her lower lip. "I plan on going to graduate school."

"I know, and if you need me to watch her more so you can go to classes or study, I gladly will."

She'd been afraid of that. "Well, there's something you don't know."

"What is it?" He waited for her answer.

"About graduate school..."

"Yeah?"

"I planned on going to the University of Miami." He blinked. Twice.

The waiter set steaming plates in front of them both, but she didn't look away from Tom. She murmured a thank-you to the waiter. Tom's face reddened. She braced herself. *Here it comes.*

"Florida?" The vein in his forehead throbbed. She couldn't look away from it. "You've known this—and you didn't tell me?"

Put like that… "Yes."

He unfurled his napkin to the side and slapped it into his lap. "What else aren't you telling me? What else have you kept from me? Let's add them up, Stephanie." He lifted his index finger. "A boyfriend. A daughter. A cross-country move. What else? You haven't shocked me enough." He bent his fingers in a come-here gesture. "Bring it on."

All the guilt she'd carried for the past five years pressed against her, but the mention of a boyfriend snapped it like a brittle twig.

"He was never my boyfriend. I told you." She grabbed her fork and started spinning it in the pasta. "I'll admit I crossed an emotional line with Aaron, but he was never my boyfriend. We didn't even kiss."

"Well, terrific. I'm glad you never kissed him. It makes me feel better that you spilled all your secrets to him while you lied to me."

"Stop it." She leaned forward, glaring. "It's over. It's in the past. I told you I was wrong, that I was sorry. It's obvious you'll never let it go. Sew me a scarlet letter, Tom. Go ahead. But believe me, I have already paid. Oh, how I have paid."

"You haven't paid the way I have. Not even close."

His eyes smoldered, accusing, burning.

She slapped her fork back on the table. As if his life was so tough. Managing a profitable company, never worrying about money. Having tons of free time to train. "I can barely keep my head above water. I have to wake up at five-thirty to get myself and Macy ready, drive her to a day care I can barely afford, rush to a job I find boring, then sit through school for a few hours, pick up Macy, make dinner, play with her and find time to study. I'm so exhausted at night I can barely sleep."

He sat there, a granite block.

Her shoulders dropped. Why had she blurted all that out? She wasn't one for pity parties. She'd accepted the blame, taken it, worn it and owned it because it was hers. *When will it be enough? When can I let go of this guilt?*

What about the Bible passage she'd read over and over? In Isaiah. The one where God blots out sins and never thinks of them again.

Did You blot this one out, too, Lord? If You don't think of it again, why can't I stop thinking about it?

"We both paid," Tom said without a trace of bitterness. "But it didn't have to be that way."

"No, it didn't. But we can't change it. And if we can't spend an hour together without arguing, I wonder if any schedule we make will work. What kind of example will we be setting for Macy?"

"You're right." He nodded to her plate. "Go ahead and eat before it gets cold."

"I'm not very hungry."

He tapped the table with his knuckles. "I'm trying, Stephanie. It's hard to work through this when new information—life-changing information—keeps getting dropped in my lap. I've only had a few weeks to process this. Put yourself in my shoes."

She ducked her chin, tried to be reasonable. "I'm not being fair. I know. But my life is changing, too, and I'm scared, okay?"

Neither spoke. The ambient noise of the restaurant whispered around them. Stephanie's food smelled delicious and garlicky, but she couldn't bring herself to take a bite.

Tom didn't touch his food, either. "Tell me now, is there anything—anything you can think of— that I should know? I don't know where to go with this whole Florida thing, but before I think about it, I have to be sure I'm not going to have another nuclear bomb explode on me."

Stephanie gave her head a small shake. "No, Tom. You know everything."

"Then let's finish our meal and work out a schedule for now."

She finally picked up her fork, but worries kept buzzing around her head. A big one gained momentum, until she finally gave voice to it. "If we're doing this, I'm not going to be the wife."

He gave her a quizzical look.

She continued, "I'm not calling or texting to remind you that 'tonight's your night' or 'don't forget about such-and-such.'"

"I didn't ask you to."

"Yeah, but that's what these arrangements turn into. I don't have the time or desire to role-play. If there's a special event, I'll email you the address and time, nothing more. You're responsible for remembering it. And if you don't, you can explain it to Macy."

"No one asked you to be my secretary. I'm a grown man. Give me the information, and I'll be there." He tilted his head slightly. "While we're on the subject of things we will and won't do, then I'm asking you to at least consider applying to graduate school here. I'm Macy's dad. Not for a couple of months. For good."

"I'll think about it." Just uttering those words sent a shiver over her skin. Her goals, her dreams were already fading. She drew her lips together.

She'd work out the visitation schedule and consider what was best for Macy, but she wasn't going to become an afterthought in her own life. Not ever again.

Chapter Seven

Tom looked at his reflection in the rearview mirror. Clean-shaven, hair more tidy than usual. He checked his tie. Straight. As ready as he was going to be.

Stepping out of his truck, he straightened the legs of his dress pants, then reached over and grabbed a large wrapped present before shutting the door. His feet barely made a sound as he walked up the sidewalk to Stephanie's apartment. The moon had already slid into place, shining bright and full in the black sky. He inhaled the cold air. It tasted good. Like winter. Fresh.

Stephanie buzzed him in, and, with jittery nerves, he climbed the stairs to her door.

Tonight was the night. They were telling Macy.

God, give me the right words. We're about to change this little girl's world, and I don't want to scare her. Open her heart to me. Please, Lord, make this easy on her.

He inhaled. Exhaled. Knocked on the door.

Stephanie opened it, and his mind blanked. Stunning. The chocolate-brown sweaterdress hugged her waist and dropped over her hips, revealing brown tights and tall boots. Her hair fell in loose waves around her shoulders, and her lips were darker red than normal. He met her gaze— as terrified as his.

She blinked rapidly. "Come in. Why don't you sit at the table while I get Macy?"

Macy flew down the hallway, her arms wide. "Tom!"

He put the present on the floor, caught her and boosted her in the air, choking up at this unexpected display of affection. "Hey, munchkin, how are you tonight?" He set her on her feet.

"I'm good. Do you like my dress?" She swayed this way and that, the purple skirt swishing around her knees. "Mommy said tonight is special, so I wore my fancy dress."

"I love it. You look magnificent."

"What's that?" She pointed at the present he'd set on the floor.

He grinned. "It's for you, but your mom and I want to talk to you before you open it."

A frown crossed her face, but she quickly brightened. "Is it a cash register? I've always wanted one of those."

Tom met Stephanie's twinkling gaze over

Macy's head. She shrugged. He made a mental note to add a cash register to his Christmas list.

"Let's sit down." Stephanie herded them to the table.

He'd stopped by three times since their heated lunch meeting, and they'd settled into a truce. He'd made himself a promise not to bring up the past anymore. Not the bad parts, at least. Prayed each night about it, too. So far, he'd succeeded. And he'd been enjoying her company. In fact, he grew more impressed with her each hour they spent together. Stephanie was a terrific mother— loving, nurturing and not afraid to discipline.

They'd also agreed on a schedule with Macy and taken the steps necessary for him to have joint custody. His lawyer was hammering out the child support arrangement. The friend of the court papers had been filed.

Thanksgiving was two days away—the day they had agreed to introduce her to his family. He couldn't wait. But first he and Stephanie had to be honest with Macy, and he'd asked Stephanie to take the lead.

"Macy, I told you tonight is special, but I haven't explained why." Stephanie folded her hands and rested them on the table. "I have something to tell you. It's why I asked Tom to come over."

Macy's eyes grew round, and a smile spread on her face. "Are you getting married?"

Tom did a double take. He hadn't been prepared for that question.

"No," Stephanie sputtered. "No, that's not it."

"Oh." Her face fell.

"You know Tom is an old friend of mine, right?"

Macy nodded.

"Well, he's more than an old friend. He used to be my husband, a long time ago."

"He did?" Macy's eyelashes curled up to her eyebrows. "Why isn't he now?"

Tom said a silent thank-you that Stephanie was handling this conversation, because he wouldn't know where to start.

"That isn't important." Stephanie shot him a helpless look. "Look at Tom's eyes, Macy. What do you see?"

"Blue. Just like mine!" Her face beamed again.

"That's right. Just like yours. Do you know why? Because Tom gave you those eyes."

Macy scrunched her nose. "No, he didn't. You can't give eyes away."

At Stephanie's nervous laugh, Tom decided it was his turn to enter the conversation. "What your mom is trying to tell you, Macy, is you have my eyes because I'm your dad."

Her little jaw fell to her chest, and he could practically see the thoughts spinning in her mind.

"You're my dad?" she asked, her tone awestruck.

He nodded and smiled. "Yes, I am."

"Why didn't I have a dad before now, Mommy?" She turned her attention to Stephanie.

"Because Tom and I broke up before you were born, and he didn't know about you." Her face strained as she said the words. A pang of pity touched Tom's heart. *God, I need to forgive her, don't I?*

"But he knows me now, so I get a daddy, right?" The hope and anticipation lighting Macy's face filled Tom with love. Her reaction was everything he'd wanted and more.

"That's right, Macy," he said. "I've always wanted a daughter exactly like you. I'm very, very happy you're my little girl." He kneeled before her, and she fell into his arms, wrapping her tiny hands around his neck.

"Can I call you Daddy?"

"I'd love that." He kissed her baby-soft cheek.

"Are you going to live here now?" She pressed her hands against his face.

"No, princess. I have my own home."

"But…" Her arms dropped to her sides. "But mommies and daddies live together."

Stephanie joined them, running her hand down

Macy's hair. "Not always, baby. Sometimes they live apart."

"But how will I see you?" Her lips trembled and tears pooled in her eyes.

"I'm going to visit you every week, and you're going to stay with me sometimes on weekends."

"Without Mommy?" Her voice broke.

He fought against the ache pinching his soul. "Just you and me. But did you know you have a whole bunch of aunts and uncles?" He lightened his tone.

"I don't want to stay without Mommy."

"I know this is new to you, so maybe you could come over to my house with your mom until you're ready to stay by yourself. Does that sound better?"

She nodded. "Can I open the present?"

"Yes, you can open the present." He straightened and walked to the door where he'd left the package. He carried it to the couch. Macy and Stephanie joined him.

Macy ripped open the paper, then lifted the cover off the box. "What is it?"

"What do you think it is?"

"It's a pirate box."

"Close. It's a treasure chest." He pointed to the lid. "Open it up." He caught Stephanie's questioning glance and winked.

Macy opened the lid of the hinged wooden

box and gasped, her hands covering her mouth. "Look at all the presents!"

She pulled out strands of sparkly beads, pretend diamond rings, a tiara, a star-shaped wand and a pen with a pink poof on the end. Then she lifted two wrapped presents. The first one was a children's Bible. She clutched it to her chest. The second was a framed picture of them taken at Chuck E. Cheese's. The frame said, "Me and My Dad."

"You're my treasure, Princess Macy."

Her face glowed, and she hugged him again. Then she ran over to Stephanie, the Bible in one hand, the frame in the other. "Thank you for my daddy, Mommy! Look at my book! Look at my fancy crown!"

"Wonderful," she said in a chipper tone. "How nice. Did you thank Tom—I mean, your dad?"

"Thank you, Daddy!" She smacked a big kiss on his cheek. Not shy at all. "I can't wait to tell Grandpa I have a daddy!"

"Well, you'll see him tomorrow night," Stephanie said. "He's staying with us until Sunday. And you're going to meet some more of your new family in a few days at Thanksgiving, too. Right, Tom?"

"That's right. In fact, you have another grandpa."

"No. I only have one grandpa." Her chin rose, and her stubborn tone came on.

Tom scrambled to come up with a solution. "Would you be willing to have another grandfather, like a papa?"

"A papa?" She lifted two sets of beads over her head. "What's that?"

"Since you already have a grandpa," he said, "maybe when you're ready, you could call your other grandfather Papa?"

"Okay." She dug into the treasure chest again, lifting all the plastic rings, bracelets and hair accessories out and shoving them on her body. "But I don't want no mean old papa."

Stephanie chuckled. "What makes you think he'd be mean?"

"No one is as nice as my grandpa."

"Your new papa is very nice, but whatever you say, Macy." Stephanie shook her head. "I'll get some drinks and snacks for us." She left the room.

"Come here a minute and bring your Bible." Tom sat on the couch and gestured for her to join him. Macy brought it over and hopped onto his lap. "Today is special to me, and I want it to be special for you, too."

She stared into his eyes, her face open, expectant.

"I'm thankful, and David, a man who lived way back before Jesus was born, was thankful, too. Do you know what he did to show his thankfulness?"

She shook her head no and snuggled into his

arms. He almost closed his eyes at the beauty of it.

"He thanked God. The Bible says he praised God with thanksgiving and song. We're going to read part of this book together whenever you stay with me. Would you like that?"

"Yay!" She clapped. "Let's read some now."

"Okay. How about we start at David's story."

As she leaned her cheek against his arm and chest, he savored the sensation of her trust. Macy asked about Goliath and what kind of name Bathsheba was. He chuckled, trying to answer her as best he could. Reading the story, it struck him how imperfect David was, yet God forgave him. Faith. A funny thing.

Tom handed the book back to Macy. *Lord, You forgave David. I'm no better, and neither is Stephanie. If You can forgive murder, I can forgive a lie.*

Peace spread from his heart, expanding, filling the pockets of guilt he'd kept open too long. And forgiveness wasn't hard. Not at all.

"So how did it go last night?"

Stephanie blew across the top of her coffee at the Water Street Coffee Joint, her favorite café in town. Bea rummaged through her purse on the table topped with colorful mosaic tiles. Light filled the space from the abundance of windows, and the sage-green paint contrasted cheerfully with the exposed brick wall. The place was packed. Stephanie let out a pleased sigh that the dentist office closed a day early for Thanksgiving. A day off—without classes or work—was what she needed, although she did feel guilty for sending Macy to day care.

"Honestly, Bea, last night surpassed my highest expectation. Macy adores Tom and is already calling him Daddy. She took it in stride, but—" Stephanie frowned "—she did ask if we were getting married and if we were all going to live together."

"Ah, the innocence of a four-year-old." Bea applied lip balm, tossed the tube in her purse and cupped her hands around her hot tea. "And you worked out the custody arrangement?"

"Yes. It wasn't complicated. We're waiting to talk to a friend of the court. When the judge signs off on it, everything will be legal."

College students and professionals ambled past the windows, some stopping to come inside. The air where they breathed poofed visible clouds.

"Sounds like Tom handled things maturely. I hear so many stories of revenge and backstabbing, to see you two working together is refreshing."

Stephanie propped her elbows on the table and

held her cup close to her mouth. "We've both matured. So far, he puts Macy's needs before his own."

"What about yours?" Bea dunked her tea bag twice before taking it out of the mug and setting it on a napkin. "Are you sensing any payback?"

She shook her head. "He asked me to consider local graduate programs."

"Really? How do you feel about that?"

"Not surprised he asked." She set her cup down. "But I had it all planned. Sunshine, warm weather, help with Macy—I don't want to give it up. I miss my dad. No offense, but before I told Tom about Macy, there wasn't anything keeping me here."

"I hear you, but you'd better get used to it. You'll be sharing big decisions with Tom for years to come."

The weight of the statement sank to the bottom of Stephanie's stomach. "Sharing big decisions, giving up control—I don't know if I can do it."

"Why?"

"I gave up control when we got married. And I hated who I became."

Bea broke off a chunk of a cookie and offered it to her. "Want a piece?" Stephanie shook her head. Bea popped it into her own mouth. "So this ex-husband of yours is domineering. Made you do things his way, huh?"

"No, I wouldn't call him domineering. Driven, maybe."

"He told you what to do."

"Not that, either."

"What am I missing?" Bea drummed her fingernails against the table. "Why did you give up control?"

Stephanie stared straight ahead but didn't focus. The past came back in the form of impressions, feelings, regrets. "He didn't control me, Bea. I gave up on myself." She sipped her coffee. "I think a part of me went into our marriage for all the wrong reasons."

"It's common." She nodded, her gaze understanding.

"College at the time was such a struggle. My grades were terrible, but my roommates got As without studying. I kept up with them by going to parties and having fun, but deep down I knew I should be sitting at a desk, doing homework. A part of me worried it wouldn't matter—I wasn't smart enough even if I did study nonstop. After we got engaged, I didn't want to deal with it anymore—the worry, the anxiety—so I quit."

"Do you think marrying Tom was a way out for you?"

"Yeah, I do. Not having to keep up with school? A huge relief."

Bea broke off another cookie piece. "You were young. What did you do all day? Did you get a job?"

She warmed her hands around the mug. "No. I should have. I had too much time on my hands. I always thought not working, not going to school, having unlimited free time would be liberating— the ideal. But it wasn't. Not at all. It was boring and lonely."

"So I'm assuming Tom worked and wasn't around during the day."

"Or at night. His dad handed him the reins of one of the family car dealerships, and he had something to prove."

"I'm guessing you were a little depressed," Bea said. "Do you still see yourself as that girl?"

"Goodness, no!"

"Are you afraid you'll use Tom as a crutch now that he's back in your life? If the custody arrangement works and Macy gets a father out of the deal, would it be so terrible to stay here a few more years?"

Yes. It would be terrible. But not for the reasons Bea was suggesting. The more Stephanie saw Tom and Macy together, the more she respected him. And the more she respected him, the more attractive he became. She'd been fascinated by him since the day they met. Attraction led to things like not moving to Florida. Or deciding her master's degree could wait. Taking the easy way out.

Or even scarier things.

Like love.

Love couldn't happen. Not with Tom. Not again. Because he was making this relationship work for Macy's sake. Not for hers.

"I told him I'd think about staying. I didn't make any promises." She took another drink, more than ready for a change in subject. "Did your turkey thaw out? When did you say Mark and Shelby are coming?"

They chitchatted about holiday plans, dinner preparations and upcoming chores.

"Are you nervous about spending the afternoon with Tom's family tomorrow?" Bea asked as they stood to put their coats on.

"Definitely. I know they'll hold a grudge against me. I have no idea how they'll react to Macy."

"Let me know how it goes. You can call anytime—even during dinner tomorrow. If you need me, just call."

Stephanie wrapped Bea into a hug. "Thanks. It's nice to have you on my side."

Tom scanned the last invoice, stacked it on top of the others, grabbed his coat and headed to the door. Almost seven o'clock. One hour's worth of work always seemed to take two. Didn't leave much time for running tonight. And with the amount of food he'd be eating tomorrow at Thanksgiving dinner, he'd be smart to run an extra mile.

He steered his truck onto Ridge Road. Hard to believe the sun had already gone down. Another sign winter had arrived.

Making a right turn, he passed Mrs. Matthews's two-story house with windows glowing like watchful eyes. She'd been his Sunday school teacher. His big mouth, lack of patience and habit for mischief had earned him her extra attention. She'd set him straight many a time with a simple glower, the look that said, "If your mama was alive, she'd be disappointed."

His mom, with her exuberant laugh, quick temper and constant hugs, had died when he was ten. The doctors had delivered Libby safely, but his mom suffered a postpartum hemorrhage. She didn't survive the birth. The loss of her would always sting.

I still miss you, Ma.

The most important women in his life left him. He couldn't prevent one from going. No stopping death. But the other?

His mind drifted back to a moment—must have been early spring, the tulips were out. With a stack of procedure manuals under one arm, he'd unlocked the door to the apartment and stepped inside, another late night trying to make sense of a complicated business. Music greeted him, one of those slow sappy songs Stephanie loved. She danced into the living room, stopping when she saw him. Her face had radiated joy. Giving him an impish smile, she'd taken his hand and tugged. "Come on, let's dance."

He tightened his hold on the steering wheel. *No. No memories. Not now.* The driveway came into view, and he blew off the images in his head. But he couldn't get rid of the feeling of that moment—the sense of possibility that slipped away with his carelessness.

Would he still be married if he had just dropped the books, wrapped his hands around her waist and danced? Kissed her? Appreciated having a wife?

He braked to a stop, cut the engine, loosened his tie and trekked up the porch into the house. Empty. Bryan must be working late or out with one of the guys. After flicking on a light, Tom changed into his workout clothes. Then he stretched, jumped on the treadmill and programmed his workout. The *swish, swish* of the belt moving signaled go time, and he settled into a rhythm.

More scenes flooded back. Stephanie reading

on the couch. A table set for one with his dinner on the plate, cold from sitting out. Tiptoeing into the bedroom after poring over invoices for hours. Stephanie's hair fanned on the pillow.

He increased the incline and pushed his legs harder. He didn't remember regretting his actions at the time. He'd honestly thought he was on the right track. Doing the responsible thing. Working hard to build a life.

But he'd missed the wife in front of him. And he didn't know it until it was too late and she was gone. Taking her beauty, music, dinners and all he loved with her.

He cranked the treadmill to eight; his legs fumbled to keep up. *God, I kind of understand why she didn't tell me about Macy. I barely paid attention to Stephanie and she was my wife.*

Last night would go down as one of the best in his life. Hearing Macy call him Daddy? Choked him up thinking about it. He no longer doubted he could be the father Macy needed. But the co-parent Stephanie deserved?

He'd botched their marriage. He wouldn't botch this.

Chapter Eight

A car rumbled up Aunt Sally's driveway, but Tom dropped the edge of the curtain when he recognized Sam's SUV. He peeked out the window again. Nothing. He was worse than a kid.

When he told the family he'd invited Stephanie, her dad and Macy to Thanksgiving, they'd acted excited, but none had successfully hidden the concerns in their eyes. He and Claire texted most days, so he knew she'd be fine. But Libby and Sam hadn't been around much, and Bryan clammed up every time Tom mentioned Stephanie. How would they all react to his ex-wife and child?

"There you are." Hands in his pockets, Dad ambled toward him, then stared out the window at the vast lawn complete with pine trees and the occasional birch. A cardinal flew from one tree to the next. "Nervous?"

Tom shifted to face him. "Yes."

"Don't be." He patted Tom's shoulder. "We'll make them feel welcome. What's past is past. We can be thankful for right now. I still wish you'd have let us get Macy some gifts, though. This is my granddaughter we're talking about." He grinned.

"Plenty of time for gifts at Christmas, Dad." Tom's insides tightened. Stephanie had requested no presents, but it was one of the ways his family showed they cared. Would they hold that against her, too? "It's going to be overwhelming enough having her meet everyone. Macy won't be used to all these adults." He hesitated. "She might not be real happy to meet everyone, either. For such a small person, she's got a big stubborn streak."

"Stubborn? She's a true Sheffield, then." He chuckled.

"Don't be offended if she doesn't warm up right away. When I mentioned her having another grandpa, she told me in no uncertain terms she had one grandpa and that was that."

Dad jostled the keys in his pocket. "I've got time. And patience."

"Do you mind if she calls you Papa?"

An odd expression twisted his face. "Papa?"

"Yeah. I thought she might be more receptive

to you if she could call you something other than what she calls Ken."

"I don't care if she calls me Grumpypants or Dale. I just want my grandchild in my life."

A flash of white next to Sam's SUV caught Tom's eye. His hands grew slick with moisture. Wiping them on his pants, he strode to the front door. Dad followed close behind.

"You made it." Tom stood in the frame and clicked a mental snapshot of the moment. Stephanie, impeccable in her wool coat belted at the waist. Her dad, Ken, glowering next to her. And Macy with a puffy skirt peeking under her coat, revealing white tights and shiny black shoes.

"Daddy!" Her face lit, and she opened her arms wide. After giving her a hug, Tom picked her up and kissed her cheek.

"Happy Thanksgiving, Macy. I see you're all dressed up and ready for turkey." Still carrying Macy, he stepped aside to let Stephanie and Ken inside. "Mr. Baynes, nice to see you. Thanks for coming."

"Call me Ken, Tom." He shrugged out of his coat and thrust it to him. "We aren't strangers."

"I'll take your coat, Ken." Dad held out his hand. "Glad you could make it. It's nice to see you again, Stephanie."

"Dale." Ken nodded. Stephanie handed Dad

her coat, too, and stood in the hallway with a pained look on her face.

"Macy," Tom said, still holding her. "This is your other grandfather."

"Papa?"

"Yes. Or you can call him something else if you'd prefer."

She wiggled and Tom set her down, but she kept one arm around his leg.

Grinning, Dad bent and held out a hand. "You're even prettier than I imagined. Welcome to the family, Macy."

She gingerly placed her fingers in his palm.

"I'd ask for a hug, but maybe it's too soon. If you're up for one later, we can try it. I won't bite, I promise." He winked.

Tom leaned to see her face. A small grin flashed and disappeared. He helped take her coat off. A pink sweater topped the black skirt.

"Let's get out of the entry. Follow me." Tom waved and led them to the enormous kitchen, where his sisters, their husbands, Uncle Joe and Aunt Sally were moving around in a frenzy. The kitchen opened to a large family room and dining area, and a huge stone fireplace climbed the tan walls. Everything about Aunt Sally's house felt comfortable. The television blared a football game, and the enticing aroma of turkey, stuffing and pumpkin pie filled the air. This was what Thanksgiving was all about.

"Ooh, turkey's almost done." Aunt Sally didn't look up from where she bent over the oven with a turkey baster in hand. "Libby, did you check those potatoes?"

"Mashing them as we speak."

"A-hem." Tom waited. They all stopped what they were doing, and one by one dropped their utensils and stepped forward.

"Macy!" Aunt Sally swept her into her arms and kissed the top of her head. "Let me get a look at you." She stepped back, tears swimming in her eyes. Her face looked about to burst open her smile was so big. "You look just like your daddy. Oh, my." She turned and dabbed at her eyes.

Macy tightened her hold on Tom's hand. "Why's she cryin'?"

"She's excited to meet you."

Claire and Libby introduced themselves and their husbands to Macy and then greeted Stephanie and Ken.

"Stephanie," Libby said in a neutral tone.

"Hi, Libby. Tom told me about your good news. Congratulations. This must be your husband."

"Yes, this is Jake. Jake, Tommy's ex-wife, Stephanie."

Tom cleared his throat and threw Libby a warning glare. She mouthed, "What?" And he narrowed his eyes at her. Of all his siblings, he worried about Libby and Bryan treating Stephanie badly. Claire would act like an adult, but those two?

Claire bent to Macy's level. "Do you like the zoo? You should come visit me sometime. I work there."

"You do?"

"Yep. What's your favorite animal?"

"Bunnies." Macy pointed to the necklace dangling over her sweater. "See."

"I love bunnies, too," Claire said. "Do you like otters?"

"What's an otter?" Macy let go of Tom's hand.

Claire led her to the island, where she was cutting pies, and boosted Macy to sit on the counter. "Help me with these pies and I'll tell you all about them."

Tom led Stephanie and Ken to the family room, where they all got settled. Bryan, Sam and a handful of cousins took a break from their football game to say hi. Dale asked Ken how his flight was, leaving Tom and Stephanie sitting next to each other on the couch in silence.

Her light perfume teased his nostrils. Flowery, feminine. His gaze fell to her dark jeans and cream-colored sweater. Classy. But she kept rubbing her thumb over her finger, and her back couldn't have been more rigid.

"What's wrong?" he murmured.

She lifted her gaze to his. "Nothing."

He tapped his hand on his thigh. "How was Macy yesterday? Did she have more questions?"

"No, nope, she didn't. She's delighted to have a dad."

He frowned. To have a dad? Or to have him as a dad? "Well, good."

"It's strange. Being here again." She scanned the room. "Brings back memories."

"Any good ones?" The question slipped out.

She lowered her chin. "A few."

"You know, when we were together?" The words tripped over each other. "Well, most of my memories of us together were good." He kept his voice low. The past pressed against his chest, his heart craving the release of honesty. All the times he'd blamed her for ruining his life had overshadowed one big fact: he'd loved her, loved being married to her, and those days, for him, had been good.

"Most of them?" She picked at the edge of her sweater.

"Until we fell apart."

"Are you sure your memory isn't tricking you?" Her tone held no trace of sarcasm.

"It's not. I might not have been what you needed, but that time was special for me." He grazed her hand.

She glanced at him, questions in her eyes.

"I know we can't go back," he said. "I just wanted you to know. I was happy being married to you."

"Mommy, what's this red stuff?" Macy whispered loudly into Stephanie's ear.

"Cranberry sauce." Stephanie pointed to the pretty serving dish filled with fuchsia jelly and bits of orange. "Would you like to try some?"

She shook her head.

"How about some turkey and stuffing? You like those. And a roll." Stephanie accepted the bowl of mashed potatoes, dished herself out some and dolloped a small amount on Macy's plate before passing it to Ken on her left.

"So, Stephanie," Sally said. Stephanie's muscles tightened. Here it came. Question time. "What brought you back to the area?"

She finished chewing the delicious turkey and sipped her water before answering. "I enrolled in college again."

"That's wonderful." Sally's dangling cornucopia earrings made a tinkling noise. "What are you going into? And how long will it be until you have your degree?"

Her tension lowered at Sally's welcoming vibe. "Accounting. I have one more semester left."

"I sure am proud of her." Her dad buttered his roll. "I can't wait to be here when she graduates."

"Thanks, Dad." She squeezed his hand. Having him there by her side gave her strength. More than he knew.

"And once she has her degree, I'll be seeing a lot more of her. And of this kiddo, too."

Stephanie froze. *No! Not here. Not now. Don't say it, Dad!*

"Why's that?" Sally scooped green bean casserole onto her plate.

"She and Macy are moving in with me down in Florida so she can get her master's degree."

The room stilled. Not a breath, not a clang of silverware on china, not a word of conversation. Dead silence.

Then Libby grunted. "Florida. With Macy."

"Libby," Tom warned. "Stay out of it."

"You knew about this?"

"Yes." He flashed a silent apology to Stephanie, then stared at Libby again, as if daring her not to say another word. She finally looked away, stabbing a yam with her fork and shooting a glare at Stephanie.

"Want me to cut your turkey?" Stephanie asked Macy in a normal tone, but inside her heart crackled. Libby hated her, and why not? If their roles were reversed, who was to say she wouldn't react the same way? All they saw was the girl who'd broken their brother's heart, the selfish woman who'd hidden a child from him, the terrible shrew who was taking their new niece to Florida like some sort of kidnapper.

Slowly the conversations resumed. Even Macy chatted with Tom.

Stephanie picked at the food on her plate, her appetite gone. It was nice of Tom to invite her here, but she didn't fit in with these people. Maybe she never had.

Tom caught her eye over Macy's head. His gaze asked if she was okay. She nodded, averted her eyes, blinking back a tear. Why did he have to be so nice? Why did he go out of his way to include her and her father? Why had he said those generous words to her on the couch?

Did he really feel that way? Had most of his memories been good? The way he'd said it made her believe he spoke the truth. But how was it possible? When she'd been such a disaster?

Her memories weren't good. She remembered being lonely, feeling like a failure, searching for fulfillment in all the wrong places. How could their perception of the same time be so different?

And why did Tom say he hadn't been what she needed? She'd been drawn to him because he was steady. Had eyes only for her. With a big, welcoming family, he'd made her feel as though she belonged. And there was no denying he protected her. Always kept to her side in crowds. Double-checked the locks each night. During their marriage she'd assumed he preferred working to being with her. But now she was Macy's provider, and Stephanie understood the pressure work brought.

Maybe Tom had been exactly what Stephanie needed, but she hadn't had the faith to see it.

"I'm full." Macy pushed her plate back.

Stephanie dug her fingernails into her palms to get her emotions back under control. "You barely ate. Why don't you eat some potatoes?"

Macy's face scrunched. "Do I have to?"

"Did you try them?"

"No."

Stephanie pointed to her plate. "Aunt Sally is a fabulous cook, Macy. Did you know she and Uncle Joe own a restaurant?"

"They do?" Macy looked across the table at Sally and Joe.

"We sure do, honey." Sally nodded, a wide smile on her face. "We'll fix you up a great big burger or some chicken tenders sometime when you're visiting your daddy. How does that sound?"

"I like chicken tenders."

"I thought you would."

Joe split open a roll. "We've got a deck behind

the restaurant, too. You can dangle your toes in there for the fish to nibble on."

She flashed a terrified glance at Stephanie.

"Don't go scaring her, Joe." Sally swatted at his arm. "Those fish don't want your feet, Macy. He's teasing."

"Have you been on a pontoon boat?" Dale angled his head to address Macy. "You and your mom can come for a ride in the summer."

Stephanie met Dale's eyes, and he nodded to her, kindness oozing from him. Her throat tightened. "Thanks, Dale, that would be nice."

She turned her attention to her food. Too bad she wasn't hungry. Sally really was a wonderful cook. And Dale had always welcomed her. Claire had, too.

But that was the problem. Their compassion made her want to forget she'd never be a part of their family again. She only had to peek at Libby to remind herself why. Next time, Macy would have to come by herself. Stephanie didn't mesh with the Sheffields even if her daughter did.

"Can I talk to you a minute, Steph?" Tom waited until Claire, Libby and Sam wrapped Macy into a game of Candy Land after dinner before catching Stephanie alone in the kitchen.

"Sure."

"Let's go out here." He waited for her to slip

on her boots before guiding her outside to the backyard. He carefully shut the door behind them. Dusk was falling, throwing shadows on the ground and pastel colors low in the sky. This time of day brought deer to the edge of the woods. He searched for them but didn't see any. "Sorry it's cold out here, but this won't take a minute."

Stephanie faced the woods beyond the yard. He wanted to go to her, to put his hands on her shoulders, touch that fuzzy sweater. Crazy. Too many memories kicked around with her in his territory. He put his hands in his pockets and stood beside her.

"Thanks for coming. I know Libby can be a real pain, and I'm sorry."

"They're protecting you." She shrugged. "I don't blame them."

"I've been thinking a lot, Steph." He stared ahead. "Before I found out about Macy, I assumed I'd made peace with the divorce and everything. But I realized I might not be as moved on as I thought."

Her questioning glance prodded him to continue. "It was good of you to come today, to share the holiday with us. It means a lot to me and to my family. They've all been excited to meet Macy."

"It was the least I could do. I'm surprised, really."

"About what?"

"They're so pleasant. I didn't exactly leave a good impression, and I'm sure the news about Macy lowered it to sewer levels."

Normally he would take her admission as a point he was right that his feelings were justified, but not this time. It kicked up the sour cranberry taste in his mouth, the way he'd used her guilt. "I think you need to let it go, Stephanie."

"Let what go?" Her words came out barely above a whisper. What was in her eyes? Fear?

"Let go of the guilt. Neither of us can change the past, so let's move forward without all the baggage."

"But I—"

He held his hand up. "An accident led you to tell me about Macy. God worked it out."

"Tom, I don't deserve—"

"None of us do. None of us deserve anything. You know the Bible verse where all have sinned and fall short of the glory of God? It means all of us. We all have sinned. Me included."

She rubbed her biceps. "That's not what I meant."

He stepped closer. "I know what you meant. I forgive you, okay? For everything."

A tear slipped down her cheek, followed by two more, and Tom fought the urge to brush them away with his thumb. He didn't trust himself to touch her. Not now. Not after admitting all that.

She sniffed, turned to him with shining eyes, took his hand in hers and held it. Nodding, she squeezed. But didn't let go.

Side by side, holding hands, they watched the sun dip below the horizon in a flaming display of color.

Chapter Nine

Fat snowflakes drifted outside the window. Stephanie sipped her tea and ignored the form on the computer screen. So many hoops to jump through to apply to these graduate programs. Time-consuming hoops. And she didn't have time to waste. Not with final papers due for two of her classes and the holidays almost here.

Speaking of the most wonderful, stressful time of the year... Christmas music blared from the television, and Macy bounced on the couch with her doll on her lap and her backpack by her side.

"When's Daddy going to be here?" she asked for the fifteenth time.

Stephanie craned her neck to see the oven clock. "Ten minutes."

"How long is that?"

"Long enough. If you're bored, you can come color next to me."

Macy sighed, sliding off the couch in a puddle of listlessness. "Don't wanna color."

"I know, I know." Stephanie smiled. "What do you two have planned today, anyhow?"

"I don't know, but I hope we play horsey. I'm the princess and I get to ride on Daddy's back to save the bunny."

Stephanie bit back a laugh. *Interesting game. No doubt who came up with that one.* "Oh, yeah?"

"Uh-huh."

"What happens when you save the bunny?"

"Daddy throws the mean dragon out the window, and we cel'brate with a tea party. Uncle Bryan is the dragon. He roars real good."

Tom's reserved brother, Bryan? A dragon? Wonders never ceased. She tried to picture him playing and found it wasn't hard at all. "Sounds like a lot of fun."

"It is. Uncle Bryan promised he'll still come over and be the dragon when Daddy gets his new house." Macy lay on her back, kicking her legs against the couch. "Where is Daddy? Shouldn't he be here by now?"

"He's getting a new house?" Stephanie tilted her head, studying Macy. She must have gotten make-believe mixed up with reality.

"With a big yard and a swing set and a room just for me." She jabbed her thumb into her chest. "I'm a big girl now. I can have a sleepover soon.

But Daddy has to get the house first. There's no place for me to sleep 'cept the stinky couch."

Stephanie spun back to face the laptop screen, her mind reeling. Tom was buying a house? Had he assumed she was dropping her plans for graduate school and Florida? Why else move out of the bungalow he shared with Bryan?

A house. Macy wasn't ready for sleepovers, no matter how enthusiastic she sounded. Stephanie's pulse beat faster.

It's not fair. All the things I want to give my daughter, he can give her. Without a thought. I would love to have a house, but it will be years before I can even think of buying one.

The intercom buzzed and Macy raced to it. "He's here!"

Stephanie didn't turn or rise when he came inside with his usual exuberant greeting for Macy, who hung back. "You're late, Daddy. Don't ever do that again."

Frowning, he pushed his sleeve up to check his watch. "Three minutes?"

Macy stomped off to her room.

He shrugged. "Hi, Steph. What's up with her?"

"She's been ready for an hour." Her tone was accusatory, but she didn't care.

"Excited, huh?" He looked over her shoulder at the laptop. "Working on a project?"

"Yes." She shifted her legs to face him. Envy

slammed back in. She'd blame it on his perfect life to match his perfect face. And why did he smell so good? Infuriating. "Macy says you're house hunting."

"I am." His voice was smooth. Like him.

She straightened her back. "Did you assume we're staying here? That I'm not considering Miami anymore?"

His eyes darkened. "I'd like it if you stayed here. I think you should stay here. But, no, I want my own place." His lips drew into a thin line. "Are you working on any other applications besides Miami?"

"Come on, Daddy." Macy appeared at his side, pulling on his jacket sleeve. "You're here to see me."

Stephanie whipped back to the computer screen.

"I'm here to see you and your mom." His tone contained a hint of steel. Then he leaned near Stephanie's ear and whispered, "Wherever you go won't stop me from being in Macy's life."

The next thing she heard was the click of the door shutting. The heat in her veins turned to slush. She hadn't even said goodbye to Macy. She ran to the door and threw it open. They were already down the first steps, holding hands, and Macy looked over her shoulder and waved. "Bye, Mama."

Stephanie's heart twisted. "Bye, Macy. Love you." She blew her a kiss, but Macy already faced forward.

Replaced.

Stephanie slunk back into her apartment, leaned against the door and slid to her knees. Her entire apartment was on display. Tiny. A bitty dining area to the left barely fit a table for four, the living room had been overtaken by their small artificial Christmas tree, the couch and the lone chair.

The walls were white once upon a time, the carpet old and stained, and—

She let out a sob.

This apartment wasn't good enough for her baby. She sat on the floor, hugging her knees to her chest, and let the tears fall.

Tom had so much to offer Macy, much more than her.

Another sob erupted from her chest. Tom claimed he wouldn't let Macy out of his life, but he'd let Stephanie go without so much as a whimper. He'd refused counseling, barely listened to her and wouldn't budge an inch.

What did she expect? Him to love her again? He loved Macy—anyone could see it. Stephanie had no doubt he'd fight tooth and nail to see his daughter, fly to Florida on weekends if necessary.

But he couldn't even show up for a movie when they were married.

Sure, he could say how he had happy memories of their marriage, but that's all they'd been. A few good times, and he'd gotten over her. Probably in a month.

And as much as she tried to pretend otherwise, she'd never gotten over him.

"I like the fact it has two stories and a big yard." Tom carried Macy up the porch steps of the still-under-construction brick home. Dad followed, and Reed, Claire's husband, opened the door. Reed and Dad had developed the new subdivision outside Lake Endwell, and this was one of three houses they'd built on speculation.

"We added some nice architectural details, but you'd be able to pick your finishes. Flooring, cabinets and all that. This model has an open floor plan. Wait until you see the lot, Tommy." Dad's enthusiasm colored his words, and he surged inside the house. "The walking trail leads right to the lake. You have lake access, too."

Tom stopped in the foyer and set Macy down. She hugged her stuffed kitten to her chest. "Why's it so dusty?"

Dad tweaked her ponytail. "If your dad buys it, we'll clean it up good for him."

"But, Papa." Macy craned her neck to take in the huge unfinished space. "There's no carpet or couches. And where's the TV?"

He laughed. "This house isn't finished yet. You bring your furniture in when it's all done. What do you want with a TV, anyhow? You don't like cartoons, do you?"

"Yes, I do."

"Turns your brain to mush. Come on—I'll show you upstairs where the bedrooms will be." He held Macy's hand and led her up the curving staircase, keeping her between the wall and him, since no handrail had been installed yet.

Reed handed Tom a piece of paper with the specs and layout on it. "What do you think?"

Tom scanned the information, then stretched his neck to see up the two-story entryway. "So far I like it. Why don't you show me the rest of the place?"

"Your formal dining room is to the right. Leads to the kitchen. There's an office to the left. It's not big, but it'll have a nice view of your front yard. Did you notice the cul-de-sac? It'd be perfect for Macy to ride a bike around. No traffic back here."

Tom pictured Macy pedaling in circles on the bike he was buying her for Christmas, streamers fluttering out of the handlebars. He continued through the hall, passed the framed walls of a half bathroom and stopped in the living area. Windows lined the back wall, showing off a spacious backyard surrounded by trees. Private. Big.

"This is great." Tom poked around, impressed

with the size. "I see you're putting in a fireplace on the far wall."

"You could choose if you want stone, brick, tile, whatever." Reed showed him the kitchen, an empty space at this point. "Picture a large island here. You could fit four stools easily."

Tom nodded. "I'd like to see upstairs. Three bedrooms, you said?"

"And a bonus room. It could be a playroom."

They made their way upstairs, checked out what would be the master suite and the rest of the bedrooms, then returned downstairs. Dad chased Macy in a game of tag. Her giggles filled the air.

"You said this has a basement, too, right?" Tom asked Reed.

"It does."

"Good. I'd want to finish it before moving in. I need a gym down there."

"Wouldn't be a problem, Tom. In fact, I could put you in touch with a designer I know who specializes in home gyms."

"How big did you say the yard was?" Tom slid open the back patio door and stepped onto the grass.

Reed checked his spec sheet. "Half an acre. There will be a patio where you're standing, and, of course, the property will be landscaped. What do you think about the place?"

Tom rubbed his chin. He thought it was perfect.

But the dregs of the weird interaction with Stephanie that afternoon lingered. What had made her short-tempered? And why was she so intent on moving to Florida?

"It's a big place, Reed. I like it. A lot. I'll have to think about it, though."

"Sure. I've been trying to convince Claire to move out here, but so far I haven't been able to budge her."

Tom laughed. "Get my sister out of her cabin on the lake? That will be the day."

"I know, I know." Reed shrugged. "But if we're going to start thinking about a family, we'll need more room."

"Are you telling me something?" Tom searched Reed's face for any hints Claire might be pregnant.

"No. But we're thinking about it."

"That's great, man. You two would be good parents."

"How's parenting been for you?" Reed tilted his head, concern in his eyes.

"I love it. Having Macy in my life has made all the difference. She's—well, she's got me wrapped around her finger, I guess, and I wouldn't have it any other way."

"What about her mom? You two getting along?"

Tom sighed, kicking at a piece of gravel by the door. "Most of the time. She's surprised me. But I still don't know if she's moving next year or not. I'm trying to talk her into staying." She'd left him once. What was keeping her from leaving again?

Reed frowned. "You could try to block her from going. Get a court order."

He shook his head. "Not my style, Reed. We'll work it out."

"You still want a big house here in Lake Endwell if Macy won't be around?"

"Good question." His chest broadened as he studied the backyard. If Stephanie left, he'd be rambling around this huge house by himself. But he would get Macy sometimes—he'd make sure of it. A week at Christmas. A couple weeks in the summer.

Not enough. Even the few hours he had on weeknights and Saturdays weren't enough.

He drew his eyebrows together as it hit him. He wanted Macy all the time. Every day.

But he would never take her from her mother.

So Stephanie had been on edge, high-strung, earlier. It wasn't like her. Maybe she was thinking of Macy's best interests, too. Staying in Kalamazoo wasn't her dream—he knew it.

Tom glanced over at his brother-in-law. "Don't be like me. Work extra hard on your marriage. I love Macy, but sharing her is hard on both Stephanie and me."

Reed rocked back on his heels. "I don't know

what happened, so tell me to shut up at any time, but she never remarried. You act like the women around here are invisible. Any chance of you two getting back together?"

He almost choked, but the idea wasn't foreign. The minute he'd stepped inside this house, he could picture Stephanie here. Could see her brushing Macy's hair. Bending over a computer keyboard in the office. Sipping a mug of coffee on the front porch. Lounging on the nonexistent patio. Maybe she'd turn the music on. This time he'd pull her to him, dance with her. Make her feel special. Loved.

Except they weren't in love.

Tom put his hand on Reed's shoulder and looked him in the eye. "No."

He didn't have the personality to make her happy. He made her miserable, without even knowing it, once. Wouldn't make her miserable again.

Chapter Ten

As the final strains of "Silent Night" filled the church Christmas Eve, Stephanie closed her eyes and bowed her head.

Heavenly Father, thank You for sending Your perfect Son to be our Savior. For bringing Tom back into our lives. He's wonderful with Macy. Every little girl should have a dad like him.

She opened her eyes, her throat thick with emotion. Macy had fallen asleep on Tom's lap. Her red ruffled dress, courtesy of Aunt Sally, bunched up by her knees, her ringlets smooshed against his dark dress shirt and wine-colored tie. Stephanie glanced at his hands holding Macy tightly. Strong hands. Tender, too.

Macy had spent the day with him and his family. Stephanie declined the invitation to join them. Her first Christmas Eve alone. Utterly alone. No Dad, no Macy, nobody.

And it had been all right.

In fact, she'd needed the time to wrap Macy's presents and to finish up her gift for Tom.

The lights came back on, and the congregation shuffled outdoors. But she and Tom stayed.

"Tom?"

"Hmm?" He must have been deep in thought.

"It was generous of you to come to church with us. You could have had more time with her, you know."

"I know." He tightened his hold on Macy. "But church on Christmas Eve is a good tradition, and candlelight services remind me of Granddad and growing up."

She nodded, but the unspoken words wouldn't come out. He could have taken Macy to his own church in Lake Endwell with his family, and he'd chosen instead to bring Macy home and attend with her. She placed her hand on his arm. "This was the nicest Christmas gift you could have given me."

He juggled Macy to scoot out of the pew. She didn't wake, simply rested her cheek on his shoulder. "You let me have her all day. Couldn't have been easy on you."

"It was the least I could do. You're letting me take her to Florida the rest of the week." They joined the line of people in the aisle. "I appreciate you working around my classes next semester, too."

"It doesn't matter to me what days I have Macy, as long as I have her."

"It saves me a lot of hassle. I usually don't have night classes. I would have had to find a babysitter Tuesdays and Thursdays, and now I don't. Thanks."

After shaking the pastor's hand and greeting the other worshippers, they continued down the concrete steps. A light snow fell, swirling around the parking lot. Tom settled Macy into the booster seat in his truck while Stephanie sat in the passenger seat. When he started the engine, she snuck a peek at his profile.

And wished she hadn't.

He was a beautiful man. Physically and spiritually.

"Why didn't you ever get remarried?" The words were out of her mouth before she could stop them. Jingle-jangle Christmas music played from the radio station, matching her wobbly state of mind. His stunned glance brought heat to her cheeks.

"Why didn't you?" He backed out of the parking spot and turned onto the street. The residential block boasted bright decorations of Christmas lights, white wire reindeer and wreaths wrapped in big red bows. Snow collected on the ground like frosting on the cookies she'd baked that afternoon.

"I asked you first." Besides, she didn't know how to answer. She'd had many reasons over the years, but ever since Tom had come back into her life, she suspected none of them were true. She wanted to ask again, to dig it out of him, but she didn't have the right.

He peeked at her. "Seriously, Steph, why didn't you remarry?"

The striped gloves on her hands suddenly fascinated her. "I could say I didn't have time to date or that the few men who crossed my path didn't interest me in the slightest. I wouldn't be lying. It's more complicated, though."

"Oh, yeah?" He slowed for a traffic light.

The answer came to her swiftly, and she blurted it out without thought. "I needed to find myself."

Silence settled, but it wasn't chilly or off-putting. "And did you? Find yourself?"

"I'm working on it." Before he came back in the picture, she'd say she had. Miami. CPA. Success. But now? She wasn't so sure.

"Who were you when you were with me?" He cast a sideways glance her way. She didn't miss the unguarded emotion in his eyes.

"Someone who ran away when life got hard. A quitter."

"But…" He concentrated on the road.

"What?" She shifted to watch him. He swallowed.

"I don't get it. I fell in love with her, the girl you were. I never saw you that way. I didn't care you quit school. I planned on providing for both of us, anyhow. I loved who you were then."

Part of her clung to his words, but the other part mentally yelled, "Liar!"

"Can you really say that was true after we were married?"

He waved absentmindedly. "Well, yeah."

"If you say so." She sighed. "I think we were both in love with each other, but I don't think either of us were good at showing it." A sad rendition of "I'll Be Home for Christmas" came on the radio.

"I won't argue that." His words were gruff but lacked sarcasm. "I've thought back on that time a lot. I would have done things differently. Take work—I wish someone would have told me I needed time to gain the necessary skills to run the dealerships. Maybe I'd have spent more nights with you and fewer at the office. Maybe not, I don't know. I have a pretty thick head. But one thing I'm sure of—I would have worked harder to make you feel special, to make you stay."

She blinked back tears. This…this was why

she'd fallen for him back then. Why it was hard to be with him now.

She let out a weak laugh. "I figured you weren't interested because I wasn't interesting. You got a dud for a wife, and you'd learned it too late."

A horrified look crossed his face and then he laughed, quieting quickly after checking the mirror to make sure he didn't wake Macy. "I never thought of you as a dud. Where did you get that idea? I wasn't around because I had something to prove. I wanted to buy you a nice house, get started on a family and earn enough money to provide for you and a couple of kids."

Her heart dropped. A family, ironically, was exactly what she'd stolen from him when she left. And all he had wanted to give her then were the very things she desperately wanted now.

He continued, "Look, I respect what you're doing, going back to school and getting your degree. But none of that mattered to me. I loved you. You. Not anything more."

She twisted her hands in her lap. He spoke the truth. She could kick her younger married self for buying into the lies her imagination kept feeding her.

"I didn't feel worthy of you. I was in between. Confused."

"I know that now."

"You do?" Why did those words fill her with so much hope? Why did his opinion of her still matter?

"You've become the person you were meant to be. I give you credit for all the things you've sacrificed to provide for Macy."

She scrambled to cling to what he just said, to savor it later. "Thank you. I...well, I admire you, too."

Back at Stephanie's apartment, Tom tucked Macy into bed and joined Stephanie in the living room. Her small tree full of colorful bulbs and tinsel welcomed him. Or maybe the loving expression she'd worn all evening was to blame. Whatever tugged him to stay, he'd best ignore it. Too many familiar feelings threatened, feelings he'd declared off-limits the day he'd switched from being married to divorced. "I guess I'll be on my way."

"Wait, do you have to go now?" Stephanie's red sweater brought out the dark brown hues of her hair. "I'll make some hot chocolate. I have something to give you."

He tapped his teeth together twice. Stay and fight the attraction pulling him to her? Or slink home to the safety of his family?

"If you have somewhere to go, I won't keep

you. I just… Give me a minute." She held up a finger and raced to her bedroom.

What in the world?

She returned, her cheeks flushed and a shy expression in her eyes. "I hoped you would open it here."

A square box of a present filled her hands. Silver paper, blue ribbon and a big silver bow on top. Fancy. She'd taken her time with it. Or had it wrapped. Either way, it looked special. Why that pleased him, he couldn't say.

"I'm not in a rush." He eased his jacket off and slung it over the back of a chair.

"Good. Have a seat, I'll make the drinks and be right back." One lamp cast warm light over the room, and he relaxed into the cozy setting. The microwave dinged and within moments, she set a tall mug topped with whipped cream before him on the coffee table. She sat in the chair opposite him, holding her cup, and crossed one leg over the other. "Go ahead. Open it."

He frowned. He hadn't bought her anything. But why would he? Their relationship was no longer defined.

Lifting the gift onto his lap, he untangled the ribbon, then tore off the paper and let it fall to the floor. A large book appeared. A scrapbook. He opened it to the first page.

To Tom. The first years of Macy's life.

A picture of Macy swaddled in a blanket with the hospital bracelet still on her wrist covered most of the first page. The caption gave all her birth statistics. Time of birth, height, weight and where she was born. He traced the picture with his finger, catching his breath, unable to suppress the elation rushing through him.

He turned the page. A collage of photos smiled back at him. All of Macy as a baby. With little tufts of black hair. Big eyes. Footy pajamas with giraffes and ducks. A pink dress. There—she was smiling in that one. On all fours. Crawling. Sitting. Giggling. Messy.

Each page showed another milestone, a slightly older version of the little girl who'd captured his heart. Macy at two, crying on Santa's lap. In a sundress, blowing on dandelion seeds. Sleeping on the couch. Bare feet. Purple Popsicle grin. The pictures knocked away a worry he had never voiced.

Had Macy been okay without him? Or maybe a better way to put it—had she had a happy childhood so far?

The pictures, even the ones where she pouted, said yes, she'd been fine all this time.

When he reached the last page, he closed the book and met Stephanie's eyes.

"Do you like it?" She bit the corner of her lip.

His chest thumped. "Like it?" He gestured for

her to come over, patted the seat next to him. "It's incredible. Tell me about each picture. Tell me everything, Steph." His voice grew gravelly at the end, and he cleared his throat, but when she scooted next to him, her thigh scraping his, he fought the urge to put his arm around her. To draw her closer.

"Really? You like it?"

"Why wouldn't I? This is amazing." He shook his head again. "Thank you."

"I worried it would only make it worse. The hurt. You know, I—"

"You don't have to say anything more. This means everything to me. I can't tell you—now I have all these missing pieces."

He leaned over and kissed her cheek. Inhaled her fragrance in the process. And he forgot why he'd ever let her go.

She gave him a startled look and quickly pointed to the first picture. She told him about the day Macy was born, her words tumbling out in a nervous stream. He tore his attention from the pulse in her neck and listened to her tales of Macy. But he found himself equally fascinated by the expressions accompanying the stories.

Two hours passed before he knew it. And as he stood to leave, he pulled Stephanie to him, held her tight and whispered, "Thank you. This means more to me than you'll ever know."

Chapter Eleven

"Three days a week isn't enough, Tom." Sean scanned the chart in his hands and frowned. "It's okay for now, but you're not even up to a mile. And it's easier to swim in a pool."

Tom climbed the ladder as water dripped from him. Swimming in open water meant dealing with currents, low visibility from the murkiness and, the most erratic factor of all, the weather. If he couldn't master the pool, how would he make it through a lake with hundreds of other swimmers?

"What do you suggest?" Tom ran a towel over his hair and sat on a bench. Sean clicked his pen, scribbling on his clipboard. Snow fell in hurried pellets outside the window. The evergreens were dipped in white. A shiver rippled over Tom's skin. He wiped the rest of his body down with the towel.

"Laps every weeknight," Sean said. "We'll add distance on Saturdays."

Tom's legs splayed, his bare feet cool on the tiles. He already woke at four-thirty every morning to jog. If the weather was too icy, he ran on his treadmill. After work, he got on his stationary bike for at least an hour. Swimming he could fit in, but what about his time with Macy? Only three weeks into January and he was already struggling to balance his time with her and his training.

"I'm not sure if I can commit to that."

Sean tapped the pen against the clipboard. "You don't *have* to do anything. But you asked my opinion. If you want to finish the IRONMAN in less than twelve hours, you're going to have to put a lot more time in at the pool."

Tom stood, slinging his towel over his shoulder. "I know. I'm not trying to get out of training. I'm having a hard time juggling the pool with my daughter." He spent Tuesday and Thursday nights at Stephanie's apartment while she went to class. Macy joined him in Lake Endwell every other Saturday, but once his house was finished, he'd be taking her for the whole weekend. He'd put an offer on the new construction house Reed and Dad showed him before Christmas. The basement was being finished this week. His early-February move-in date would be here before he knew it, and moving all his stuff meant more time away from training.

Sean shrugged. "Can't her mom help out? Watch her for an extra hour so you can swim?"

"She has classes. And she works." Tom shut his mouth before he started defending her more.

"We're all busy." Sean lifted his eyebrows. "Seems to me she could accommodate you with this, but hey, I get how hard it can be to deal with an ex. What about Tot Spot? A lot of parents drop their kids off at the babysitting center here. It's fun for them."

"Babysitting center, huh?" Tom slipped his feet into his flip-flops and headed toward the locker room. Did it make him a terrible dad to consider Tot Spot? Probably.

"If you're serious about this race, you should." Sean tucked his clipboard under his arm and nodded goodbye. "See you in a few days."

Tom changed into jeans and a pullover, then asked the front desk about their child care options. He strode to the room where Tot Spot was held and peeked inside. Didn't look too crowded. Kids laughed and chased each other. Could be an option.

Out in the parking lot, he tucked his chin, bracing himself against the wind and snow. If he drove Macy to the Y with him on Tuesdays and Thursdays, he'd be able to swim every weekday.

Sure, it would cut an hour out of their together time, but he'd said all along he wasn't compromising his training schedule.

Except Macy meant more to him than a race did. Being her dad had become top priority. Still, did he have to throw out his dreams to be a good father?

On his latest Saturday with Macy, he'd tried to fit a run on the treadmill in, but she got bored of the cartoon and the book he gave her. They'd ended up playing tea party, then house, and there went his workout. And work was busier than ever. Even asking his assistant managers to take over more duties hadn't helped.

He jerked open his truck door and hopped inside, switching the heat setting to high as the engine whimpered to life. For someone dead set on finishing the race in a certain amount of time, he wasn't acting like it. Before October, he'd spent thirty minutes on the weekend planning his nutrition and meals for the week. Each day he'd charted his workout progress and planned how many miles to add to his bike routine and running regimen.

But between work and Macy and picking out fixtures for the new house…

Excuses.

He shifted the truck into gear and drove out of the lot.

When he got home, he was making a new plan. New training goals. A grocery list. Meal schedule. Nonnegotiable training chart. Tomorrow was Tuesday—he'd bring a bag with his swim gear to Stephanie's and try the Tot Spot program. One hour. Macy would fit right in with those other kids.

"I'm drowning in a sea of papers, ledgers and computer programs. Why didn't I take this class earlier? It's killing me." Stephanie dug into a low-calorie frozen dinner. She loved a hot meal for lunch in the winter, but eating out was too expensive to swing on a regular basis. The work microwave was a lifesaver. Bea sat across from her in the break room and opened her cute plaid lunch tote.

"Only a few months left." Bea unwrapped a turkey sandwich. "Think of the finish line."

Stephanie stirred the chicken and noodles and suppressed a yawn. She'd stayed up past midnight finishing the homework due tonight. "Four months. I can hold on another four months. I hope."

Bea grinned and popped a potato chip into her mouth. "You can do it. How's Macy this week?"

"Her cold is lingering, but I think she's through the worst of it. I keep giving her cough medicine, but she wakes at least once each night. I hate seeing the smudges under her eyes."

"I remember those days. Seemed like my kids would cough for weeks. Never knew if I should keep them home or send them, but what do you do? They can't take two weeks off school for a cough."

"Exactly. I'm just fortunate she hasn't had a fever. Her day care center almost sent her home Friday."

Stephanie took another bite and stared out the small window. Yesterday's snow lingered, but no new flakes fell. She missed green...or color in general. "What I wouldn't give to visit Dad right now."

Bea nodded. "I hear Miami is in the high seventies today. How close is his condo to the beach?"

"Two blocks. Wouldn't that be something? To walk two blocks to the beach? I really want to move."

Bea wiped her hands on a napkin and cracked open a Diet Coke. "Sounds like you're considering staying. Are you?"

"I don't know."

"Ah." The way Bea said it—Stephanie narrowed her eyes.

"What?"

"Tom convinced you."

"No." Stephanie sprinkled pepper on her noodles. "I'm not throwing out my plans due to peer pressure, if that's what you mean."

"All I've ever heard was how you couldn't wait to finish your bachelor degree so you could move to Florida, bask in the sunshine and spend time with your dad again. And now Tom comes back into your life and asks you to apply around here. Did you suddenly realize you like snow?" Her smile teased.

"I never said I like snow. I hate winter. I'm tired of shoving Macy's arms into a huge puffy coat every day. Scraping my windshield brings out the beast in me. Just the thought of spending two more months without a drop of color other than white, gray or brown in the landscape makes me want to weep. This isn't about the weather."

"I know it's not about the weather. It's about your ex."

Stephanie shifted her jaw. Yeah, it was about her ex. "I don't blame him for not wanting me to move. I mean, he's finally getting to know his daughter. Why would he want her to live more than twenty hours away? It seems reasonable to me."

"Sure." Bea nodded. "Tom gets his daughter. Macy gets her daddy. You can always visit Florida."

She twisted the cap off her water. No beach. No sun. No Dad. "Exactly. It's not about me."

"It should be. This is your life," Bea said. "I'm not saying you shouldn't stay, but do it for your own reasons."

"I hear you, but seeing Tom and Macy together makes me want to throw out my agenda. He's buying a house, and Macy will have her own room. He plays with her, spends time with her, loves her. If I take her away, it would hurt them both."

"Is there another reason you're thinking about staying? You could have gone to college in Miami last year if you really wanted to. Maybe Florida has never been your dream."

"Then whose would it be?" She snorted, taking another bite.

Bea didn't answer. She sipped her Diet Coke.

"I stayed here for the scholarship." Stephanie pointed her plastic fork at Bea.

"I know."

"I mean, Dad offered to pay, but…" Stephanie frowned. She still wanted to move to Miami. She did. Who didn't love the beach? Plus, moving down there would make Dad happy. She owed him for all he'd done for her and Macy.

Wait.

She *owed* him?

Maybe Bea had a point about Miami never being her dream. Florida had always been Dad's retirement goal.

"And who knows?" Bea lifted a carrot stick. "Maybe you and Tom will get back together."

Stephanie crinkled her nose and shook her head. "I don't see that happening. I already applied at Miami and here at Western. I would have to get accepted before I can make a decision."

"You'll make the right one."

She tossed her trash in the basket. Too many scenarios clamored for attention. Making the right decision had never been this hard.

Chapter Twelve

"I don't like it there, and I'm not going back." Macy crossed her arms over her chest and stamped her foot. Her big purple coat swallowed her, but the displeased scrunch of her face still shone through.

"What didn't you like about it? Scoot in so I can shut the door." Tom gently nudged her into Stephanie's apartment and closed the door behind them.

"It's stinky."

He unzipped her coat, helped her out of it and hung it up in the closet.

"Is it stinky like it smells or something else?" He collapsed onto the couch and patted his lap for her to sit on it. She lifted her chin high, arms locked against her chest, and didn't move.

"Why can't we stay here?" she asked. "You don't need to swim."

"I do need to swim. Remember? I'm going to be in a big race this summer. You don't want me to stop in the middle of the lake, do you?" He waved his arms, pretending to flounder.

She slunk to him and sat on his lap, lifting her hand to brush back the hair at his temple. "You already can swim 'cross the whole lake."

"No, I can't." He grinned. "That's why I have to swim every day."

"But I don't want you to. I don't like it there. Can't I swim with you?"

He pressed his forehead to hers. "I wish you could, sweetheart, but not when I'm doing laps. It's only an hour. We still have lots of time together."

Her lips drooped in a pitiful frown. "I don't want you to swim. I want to stay here. With Mommy."

Tom sucked in a breath as his heart sliced open. This was the first time Macy had played the Mommy card. *She doesn't mean it. She's just being a normal kid. Trying to play on my emotions.*

"You can't stay here with your mom," he said gently. "You know she's in class."

"Then I'm gonna run away. I'm taking Fluffy Bunny with me. And you'll be sad and stop swimming, and Mommy won't go to class no more."

Ah, the logic of a child. He caressed her hair. She swatted at his hand.

"Where are you going to go?" He kept his tone nonchalant.

Her nose tipped up. "Florida. My grandpa will want to see me."

"Florida is hundreds of miles away." He rubbed his chin, making a show of thinking hard. The little scamp was playing hardball. "How are you going to get there?"

"I'm gonna ride a pony. A white pony with pink ribbons in its hair and tail, just like I saw at the fair with Mommy this summer."

"Where are you going to get this pony?" Resting his chin against his knuckle, he narrowed his eyes.

"Sammie. She has ponies at her house." She frowned. "I think she does. I don't 'member."

"But if you leave, I'll miss you."

"Then you have to stop swimming." Her face, so serious, almost cracked him up.

"I'm not going to do that." Part of him wanted to give in to her demands. He hated leaving her for even an hour.

"Then I'm getting on that pony."

His patience wore thin. It was one thing to indulge her in a typical childhood fantasy and another to listen to escalating blackmail. *God, a little help here?*

"Macy, is there something you want more than anything?"

Her eyes sparkled, and she straightened, clasping her hands to her chest. "I want to be a ballerina!"

A ballerina? That could work. "You know ballerinas don't just wake up one day and can dance, right?"

She nodded, wiggling on his lap to see him better. "They go to dance school. Tatum has a leetard and a pink tutu. I wish I did." Her drawn-out sigh gave him an idea.

"Well, the race I'm in this summer is kind of like ballet. I have to train for it and get my body ready or I won't be able to finish."

"How's that like dancing?"

"Ballerinas have to take classes every week and stretch at home. Are you sure you want to be a dancer?"

"Yes!" Her eyes couldn't get any rounder or more twinkly.

"I'll tell you what." He touched the tip of her nose with his finger. "I'll find ballet lessons for you if you'll go to the Y with me so I can swim."

"Can't I go to ballet while you swim?"

Even better. "If I can find dance lessons on Tuesdays or Thursdays, then yes, I'll work it out. But you still might have to go to the kids' room sometimes while I swim."

"Okay, Daddy. What about the tutu?"

"And I'll find you a tutu. Deal?"

"I guess."

Stephanie unlocked the apartment at nine-thirty. These night classes exhausted her. Tom sat on the couch, flipping through channels.

"Hey, tough day, huh?" He rose and shoved his hands into his pockets. "Aunt Sally loaded me up with takeout for us all. There's fried chicken and mashed potatoes in the fridge if you're hungry."

"Really? You'll have to thank her for me next time you see her." She dropped her book bag and purse on the table, shimmied out of her coat and stretched her tired neck to the side. "How was Macy?" He had the look of a man who was hiding something.

"I took her to the Y tonight. She wasn't real happy about the Tot Spot program."

She pressed her hand to her temple. Tot Spot program? What was he talking about? Her body ached with fatigue.

He lifted one shoulder. "I've got to start swimming every day, so something had to give."

And Macy was what had to give? She sealed her mouth shut. She was in no condition to have this conversation. Her throat had felt raw throughout class, and all she could think about was falling into her bed.

"What? You look mad." His eyes darkened, and he stood erect, his body filling the small space. "You know this race is important to me."

"I know." She dropped into the chair, her arms dangling over the sides. Hot tea, her favorite yoga pants and her softest blanket. She was desperate for all three. "But why do you have to swim on your days with her? Can't you fit it in some other time?"

He balled his hands by his sides. She sat a little straighter. Her question was perfectly reasonable, but for some reason, he wasn't reacting well.

"No, I can't."

"Can't or won't?" Had someone rubbed her throat with sandpaper?

"I run every morning while the stars are still out. Then I haul myself to work all day. Get home, change into my sweats and hop on the stationary bike. Throw dinner together. I somehow have to fit swimming in, too. Look around." He spread his arms wide and twisted to the side. "It's winter, and the nearest pool is thirty minutes away from my house."

She brought her hand to her forehead. "I'm sorry. It's just… I already hate Macy has to be in day care all day. For her to have to basically spend another hour in day care while I'm at school?" She dropped her hand. "Why didn't I finish my degree all those years ago? I was such a dummy. And Macy is the loser."

"You're not a dummy, and Macy is okay. I don't like her in day care, either, but that doesn't mean you should quit school. I'm not giving up on my goals. It won't hurt her to see us working hard for things we want."

"She won't see it that way." Exhaustion weighed heavily on her eyes. *Bed. Sleep. Right here. Right now.*

He tapped his hand against his leg. "I think she will. She and I made an agreement."

Agreement? Guaranteed to make her life harder, whatever it was.

"She wants to be a ballerina—"

"Ugh. Not that again. I can't afford—"

"Hear me out." He thrust his palm out and gave her the smile. The devastating one capable of churning her insides to jelly. The smile that reminded her just how handsome he was.

And he was.

The muscles straining against his T-shirt didn't lie. His rumpled hair practically begged a woman to run her fingers through it—to tame it. To tame him.

"Macy and I made a deal. I'll find her ballet classes, and she'll hang out with the other kids at the Y while I swim. I'm going to try to find classes on Tuesday or Thursday. That way we'll both be happy."

Stephanie sighed, a dull ache spreading through her head. "I can't afford it."

"I'm paying for it. Along with the tutu and tights and whatever she needs."

"What if the class is on Monday?"

"I'll drive her to and from. Leave it all to me."

Leave it all to him? Yes. Nothing sounded better at the moment.

She looked up. He stood next to her. When had he gotten so close? And why did his presence send a prickly sensation over her arms?

"Are you feeling all right?" He cocked his head to the side and studied her.

She waved her hand. "Just tired. I'll be fine."

"Sure I can't get you anything before I leave? Would only take me a minute to heat the chicken for you."

"No. Thanks, though."

He swiped his coat out of the closet. "Oh, I'd better warn you. Macy claimed she was running away to Florida before we talked about ballet."

Stephanie shifted in the chair to face him. "Let me guess. She's going to Florida on a white pony with pink ribbons." She chuckled at his stunned expression. A grin spread across his face.

"Guess she's had some practice, huh?"

She nodded. "She's an old pro. Wait until you

hear her escape plan via hot-air balloon. That one's a doozy."

He laughed. "Thanks for the warning. I...I worried she might try to—"

"Run away?" She shook her head. "Don't worry. She threatens to leave when she doesn't get her way, but it's more of a coping mechanism than anything."

He turned the front door handle.

"Tom?" she said. He paused, his gaze intense. "Can I ask you something? Who do you report to at the dealership?"

He let out a half snort, half laugh. "No one. I'm the boss."

"Exactly." She circled her finger on her temple. "I'll support you if you decide to find ballet lessons, but you *are* your own boss. Doesn't that mean you can set your hours? Leaving Macy at the Y's day care isn't your only option."

He opened his mouth but didn't say anything. Then he nodded. "Get some rest, will you? You're working too hard." And he closed the door behind him.

Silly his words could be the exact medicine she needed, but they were. She changed into her favorite yoga pants, grabbed her softest blanket, brewed a cup of tea and spread her homework on the coffee table. She'd rest when the semester was over.

* * *

"Do we really get to see my room tonight, Daddy?" Macy yelled from the backseat. The basement remodel had taken longer than expected, but here it was, the second week of February, and Tom could finally move into the house. He glanced at Stephanie in the passenger seat. Her smile took his breath away.

"We sure do, princess." He winked at Stephanie. "Hope you like your new room. It's your favorite color, muddy brown."

"I don't like brown! I like pink."

"Uh-oh. I told the painters you loved brown. And orange—bright hunter's orange."

"No, no, no! I don't like yucky orange." Her voice rose an octave. "I don't want a brown room."

Stephanie twisted to face Macy. "Don't be rude. You should be thankful to have your own room."

"Wait. Did I say brown? I got it all wrong." He turned into the driveway. After opening Macy's door, he unbuckled and picked her up, careful not to slip on the ice. "I'm pretty sure there's a pink room upstairs for you."

"Really?" She kissed his nose. "It's pink?"

He nodded and carried her to the front door. Stephanie followed him.

"Wow, Tom, this is some place." Her mouth gaped open.

"You think so?" Warmth spread through his stomach up to his chest. His first house.

"Uh, yeah, I think so." She craned her neck to take it all in. "It's beautiful. All brick. And look at all the windows. Very grand."

"Thanks." He let Macy slide out of his arms, ready to bolt. "Take your shoes off first, kiddo."

She kicked off her boots and flew up the stairs.

Stephanie bent to unzip her own boots. "She's not excited at all, as you can see. Thanks for inviting me to the big reveal."

"You don't mind, do you?" He set his shoes next to the door.

"Of course not. My favorite show is *House Hunters*. I can't wait to own my own house someday." Her face lit up, and his gut clenched. *Beautiful. Confident. Stephanie.*

Everything within him wanted to offer this house to her. Which made no sense.

He strode forward. "Come on, I'll show you around."

He gave her the tour, and they ended up in the empty living room while Macy twirled around the rooms upstairs. The whole place smelled like paint and hardwood. New.

Her expression dimmed. "Macy will love it here."

What was he missing? Why the hushed words? "Why do you sound sad?"

"I'm not sad." A small smile played on her lips and she shook her head, moving toward the windows. "Well, maybe a little."

"Nothing's going to change." He tried to reassure her, not knowing how. "Macy will have her own room and a yard to play in now. No more dodging stationary bikes, treadmills and my brother. Sam is moving out of Dad's place into my old room. It's working out for all of us."

"I know." She sounded even sadder than before. What was going on?

He touched her shoulder. "Steph?"

She turned, tears glistening in her eyes. He wanted to kick himself for bringing her here and making her feel bad.

She averted her gaze, discreetly patting her eyes.

One thing he knew? He was the cause of her tears. *Great.*

"I…thought… That is, I'm…" He raked his hand through his hair. What was he trying to say? "This house was a big step for me. I finally did something for myself. On my own. Not like my job, where I fell into it. Or fatherhood, which I fell into, too. This—" he slowly spun, looking at the ceiling before fixing his gaze on her "—is something I should have done a long time ago."

"Why didn't you?"

He swallowed. *Good question.* He must have

chased her tears away, because she stared, curious, open, without a teardrop in sight.

"I think I've been waiting for something."

"What?"

He stepped closer to her. Felt her warmth. "I don't know. I was waiting for my life to change. Waiting for it to get fixed."

"Well, it certainly changed." She licked her lips. "I saw to that."

Placing his hands on her upper arms, he held her gaze. "Not what I meant. When I found out about Macy, it snapped me out of my daze. Made me realize I don't have to wait. Life is now. It's happening, and I want to live it. You know?"

She nodded. "I do know."

An invisible thread connected them. No woman had ever gotten him the way Stephanie did. None had ever listened and seemed to comprehend his chopped-up thoughts, either. He peeked at her lips. Shouldn't have.

"I'm happy for you," she whispered. "But I'm jealous, too. I want to live in a house with Macy. With a big backyard. And rooms to decorate. I'm sorry—I shouldn't be saying anything, but I want to be honest with you. No more keeping things to myself. I kept too much inside when we were married."

"I do know." His voice grew husky. "I kept

things to myself, too. If you can be honest with me, I'll do my best to be honest with you."

Her eyelashes fluttered as if she didn't know what to make of that.

He didn't, either. All he knew was the more time he spent with Stephanie, the more time he wanted to spend with her. The past was past. This was now. And now he wanted to kiss her.

"When does my bed come, Daddy?" Macy skipped down the stairs and into the living room.

Tom gave Stephanie's lips one last pining glance. "Next week, princess."

"Look, Daddy." She threw her arms in the air and spun in a circle. "I can dance in here. Miss Lotty taught me this. See? Did you see?"

"I saw. Very nice." He pretended to clap. He'd found a young ballet class that met on Tuesday nights, and so far, Macy loved it. Stephanie's comment about him being the boss had sunk in. Although not his first choice, he'd started leaving work an hour earlier each day to get his swim time in. So far, Sheffield Auto hadn't collapsed without his constant presence.

And instead of swimming during Macy's ballet class, he sat with the other parents and watched her from behind a plexiglass window. From his viewpoint, Macy was the most talented kid in the bunch.

"I'm going to leap in my room." Macy flashed a grin and raced back upstairs.

Little firecracker. He turned back to Stephanie. "What are you doing for Valentine's Day?" He hadn't planned it, but there the question was.

"I have plans." Her words flew out, and she wrung her hands.

"Oh." Why had he said anything? Now she probably thought he… What? That he wanted to ask her out on a date? Well, she'd be right. Did she have a date already? Entirely possible. He clenched his jaw. "I see."

Her cheeks flushed. "It's not a date, if that's what you're thinking. Bea and I are taking Macy to a movie."

The tension drained from him. "Oh? I shouldn't have asked. I didn't mean to put you on the spot." He reached over and loosely held her fingers in his. "It's just…this feels familiar."

She snatched her hand away. "I know. It does for me, too."

"Then what's the problem?" He scanned her face, so full of confusion.

"We had this once, Tom. It didn't work. I don't want familiar. The last thing I want is what we had."

Chapter Thirteen

Sweat dripped down the side of Tom's face as he pedaled faster, faster. *The last thing I want is what we had* replayed over and over in his head. He tried to focus on the television. The basketball game usually engrossed him but not now. Adjusting the incline, he steadied his pace.

Why had he revealed so much to Stephanie tonight? Did she have some sort of power that made him forget why he shouldn't be with her? Tempted him to look fate in the eye and spit at it, like a moron who kept swatting at a swarm of bees.

The slender body, toned legs? Part of it. Maybe her kind eyes. No, it was the smile. The elusive turn of the lips, the one suggesting a secret only he would know—that's what got him every time.

His legs tightened with each rotation. He'd better stretch his muscles after this session or he'd be fumbling around in pain the next three days. Flexibility was vital for him to continue training. Taking five minutes to loosen his legs after a cardio or strength session should be automatic, but he dreaded the twinges assuring him he did it correctly.

Flexibility, in general, didn't come naturally to him.

He'd rather push through, punish his body through a tough workout than sit still and count to eight while contorting his arms and legs.

He continued cycling, feeling the burn in his shins, calves and thighs.

What was so wrong with what they had, anyhow?

Coming home to someone who loved you. Sitting on the couch and watching a movie. Going out to dinner and laughing at each other's day. Were those things so bad?

The bike handles slipped under his sweaty hands. He grabbed the towel around his neck and wiped them again.

Memories and reality collided, and he tried to shut them out, to avoid the truth, but snippets of his married life with Stephanie kept coming back.

And he knew.

He knew why she didn't want it.

They never sat on the couch and watched a movie. They went out to dinner, but neither of them laughed. They'd eat in silence. Each caught up in their own little worlds.

If what they used to have was Stephanie's version of familiar, he agreed with her. It was the last thing he wanted, too.

"When are you and Macy moving down here?" Stephanie's dad asked. "I need to start making plans."

Stephanie's pulse tippy-tapped way too fast. Sitting on her couch after touring Tom's house, she held the phone but had no idea how to respond to her dad's question. Macy had crashed in bed the second they got home. The excitement of seeing her new bedroom had worn her out. Had worn Stephanie out, too. How could she deal with Dad when she'd already verged on a breakdown earlier in Tom's new living room?

She still squirmed about the whole Valentine's thing. Not to mention hurting him with her speech about not wanting what they had again.

He'd scared her. Unintentionally, of course, but when he'd closed the distance between them and gazed into her eyes with the look that whispered, *You, you're what I want, only you,* she'd been positive he was going to kiss her.

If he kissed her, she'd be lost.

No kissing. Not him. Too much to lose—her career goals, her desire to make decisions for herself and Macy and, most of all, her identity. Kissing him would make her want to take her whole life, throw it on the gorgeous granite counter of his brand-new kitchen and say, "Take me. I'm yours."

"Stephanie?" Dad's voice ripped her from her thoughts. "Are you there?"

"I'm here, Dad."

"How about July? Can you get everything packed by then? I'll arrange for the moving truck."

"I don't know." She'd skirted the issue with her dad for weeks. How could she tell him she was seriously considering staying in Michigan? It would break his heart. "I haven't even been accepted yet. Planning a moving date might be premature."

"Premature? Hardly." He made a scoffing noise. "You'll be accepted. I'll get the rooms set up for you and Macy. You know how she loves the beach. We'll all be together again."

"She does love the beach." Stephanie closed her eyes, picturing endless white sand. Ocean waves. Dad's happy face. "You know I applied for grad school here, too, Dad."

"Oh, that."

"Tom changes things." She crossed to the patio door. A half-moon peeked out of the clouds. Remarkably clear for such a cold night.

"You're not thinking of getting back together with him?"

"No." She shook her head even though Dad couldn't see her. "Not happening."

"Then why are you throwing your whole life away to stay there?"

Leave it to Dad to put her decisions in such an attractive light. "I'm not throwing my life away. He's Macy's father. You're the one who told me all these years what a mistake I was making for not telling him, how Tom deserved to know about his child. Well, you were right. And I was wrong, and I'm trying to make it better."

"There's better and there's smart," he said. "You think it has to be either-or, but…"

"But what?"

"But if you stay there…well, he made you miserable once. What makes you think this time would be different?"

"There isn't going to be a this time. I applied to grad school here for Macy's sake. And for Tom's."

"Hey, that sounds all nice and good, Stephanie, but don't fool yourself. You haven't gotten close to anyone since you left him. What are you going to do when he starts dating someone else? Gets re-married? Do you still want to toss out our plans?"

"He's not dating anyone."

"Oh, so that's what you're banking on."

"No!" Acid rose in her throat. Dad and Bea

should get together and take notes on how to put her worst fears front and center. They both seemed to be experts at it. "It's not my business what Tom does with his personal life. I made a huge mistake by not telling him about Macy. I'm not going to make another one by keeping them apart."

"Sounds like you made up your mind."

"No, I haven't." Why was this so hard? She pressed her fist against the center of her forehead. "I've been looking forward to moving to Florida ever since you bought the condo. I want to move down there. But I'm not saying yes or no right now. This is a big decision and it doesn't only impact me. It affects Macy and Tom. I can't make it lightly."

"I know it is," he said. "You've got to do what's best for you. And Florida is what's best. It's all you've talked about the last year."

"I know, I know." She plopped on the couch and let her neck roll back against the cushion. Actually it was all Dad talked about, and it seemed like a good plan for her at the time, but... "If I get an acceptance letter from Miami, I'll plan on visiting around Easter. I'll need to schedule an admissions interview anyway."

"You wouldn't be the first person to live in one state while your kid's father lives in another. You can still share custody and live apart."

Yeah, she could. But was that fair to Tom? To Macy?

And did she still want to?

"An anti–Valentine's Day party? You're a genius." Sam leaned in for a half embrace. "The perfect excuse to get Roxanne and Paulette off my back. Those two have more nieces, granddaughters and 'nice girls from church' than any woman on earth. Why am I saddled with two matchmakers doing administration and finances? I should hire a couple of guys."

Tom laughed. "And lose two of the hardest-working employees Sheffield Auto has? You're smart. You can handle a little matchmaking if it means keeping them happy."

"I can't handle it. Paulette set up a secret Facebook page with pictures of potential dates for me. And Roxanne tells me every day what a shame it is such a cute boy is single."

Tom led the way to the kitchen. "It *is* a shame such a cute boy is single." He lunged to the left, anticipating the punch Sam was sure to give him. Sam's fist flew past him. "Not quick enough for me, little brother."

This time Sam's hand connected with the back of Tom's head. Wincing, he rubbed it. Bryan was already in the living room. Pizzas lined the island along with a large Greek salad.

Sam let out a whistle. "How'd you get so much done? Didn't you just sign the papers?"

"I'm that good." Tom grinned. "Nah, the moving company did everything. As you can see, I have a lot to do. I don't even own pictures to hang on the walls. But you like the new sectional, don't you?" He drifted to the back of one of the charcoal-colored couches. Big pillows added pops of red, and the humongous grouping of furniture faced a big-screen TV.

Sam vaulted over the couch and lay on the chaise section, his feet crossed at the ankles. He pointed to the television. "What? Didn't they have anything bigger?"

Tom laughed. The screen ate up half the wall. "No, they didn't or I would have bought it. I like to feel as if I'm right there in the stadium when I'm watching sports."

"Any bigger and you'd be in the stadium."

Bryan came up and joined them. "I'm moving in here, Tom. I can't deal with this one." He jerked his thumb at Sam, who was still resting on the couch. "Besides, I like this bachelor pad more than our old one. You have the perfect setup."

Tom grinned, knowing he should be flattered. But bachelor pad? No. Not what he was going for with this house. "I'm grown up now. I'm done with bachelor pads."

"What are you talking about?" Sam asked as

Bryan's eyes narrowed. "Do you have a girlfriend tucked away we don't know about?"

Bryan gave Tom a sideways glance. "More like an ex-wife," he mumbled.

Tom glared him into silence. "You know I don't. But I've got Macy."

"And you're spending a lot of time with her mom, too, aren't you?" Bryan's hard stare bore into him.

"Not really." He shrugged. Depended on what was considered a lot of time. "We pass each other when I get Macy, but—"

"You brought her here the other night, didn't you?" Bryan asked.

"What, are you spying on me?"

"This is Lake Endwell, man. There are no secrets. Mrs. Daniels came in yesterday to have her car tuned up and she regaled the reception desk with the approximate time you arrived, who you were with and how long you stayed in 'the empty house with his pretty ex-wife and that darling little girl.'" The final part of his speech was spoken in a false soprano voice.

"Mrs. Daniels needs to mind her own business." Tom stalked back to the kitchen with Bryan on his heels.

"She lives across the street from you now. That's not going to happen."

Tom had forgotten how nosy neighbors could

be. In his old house, they didn't have anyone nearby to spy on them. Living in a subdivision would take some getting used to.

"Tell us the truth. Are you getting back together with her?" Bryan blocked the entrance to the kitchen, trapping Tom inside.

"No." Tom shoved him out of the way. At least he could say that with honesty.

"You want to, though, don't you? I can see it in your eyes. You're falling for her again."

"What are you talking about?" Tom tossed two slices of cheese-and-veggie pizza and a scoop of salad on a plate and sat at the table between the kitchen island and a wall of windows. He took a big bite. If his mouth was busy chewing, he could avoid the rest of Bryan's questions. His brothers joined him.

Bryan towered over Tom. "She really trapped you this time, didn't she? Are you forgetting what you went through when she left you? Because I haven't. I'm not going to sit here and watch you go through that again. Kid or no kid, you can't seriously be thinking about dating her." He waved his hand in front of him. "What does she have over you, man? She hid a daughter from you. And now she's back, and all is forgiven? What a piece of work."

"Stop." Tom jerked to his feet, the chair almost

tipping over. He got right up in Bryan's face. "You don't know her."

"And you do?" Bryan didn't back down.

"Did you ever stop and think maybe I was at fault in our marriage, too? It wasn't all her, Bryan. It wasn't. And I'm not excusing her for not telling me about Macy, but I am sick and tired of living like this." He extended his arm out.

"Living like what?" Bryan opened his hands. "What's so wrong with being single?"

"Everything," Tom blurted. "I want to see my kid every day. Not just Tuesdays and Thursdays and a weekend now and then. I want to open the door and she's here. All the time."

"It's called full custody, Tommy. You don't need a wife to make that happen."

Tom's shoulders slumped as he shook his head. Bryan didn't get it. Not at all. "Macy needs her mom. I would never separate them. Never."

"But it's okay for her to separate you? Macy needs a dad, too, Tommy. I guarantee Stephanie moves to Florida, and then what are you going to do? She's moving, and you're going to be in this big house. Alone."

"Stop it." Sam wedged himself between them and put his hand on Bryan's shoulder. "Come on—back off."

He jerked his arm free. "That's what getting married gets you, Sam—nothing."

Tom met Bryan's eyes. "This isn't about me, is it?"

"What are you talking about?" Bryan turned and marched the few steps to the kitchen. Tom followed him.

"You're scared."

"What? That's stupid. I'm not the one playing around with my ex-wife."

"No, you're not. And that's what scares you. Because if I can do it, who's to say your ex-wife couldn't come back in the picture, too, right?"

"Abby moved to Texas and got remarried. Not going to happen."

"Then what are you worried about?" Tom grabbed Bryan's arm.

Bryan wrenched free. "I'm not worried about anything! You're the one who thinks you're going forward, moving out of our house and buying this minimansion, but you're moving backward, man. You're trying to reclaim a life that's been dead for a long time."

The words pierced him, but Tom didn't flinch. He pulled his shoulders back. Clenched his jaw.

Sam looked at him, then Bryan, then back again.

"At least I'm doing something, Bryan. I sat in a funk for five years. Five years. And maybe I am trying to reclaim my life. Maybe it was dead. But why shouldn't I? I'm tired of sitting around watching ball games while everyone else gets married. They have families and live for something a little bigger than themselves. Did you ever think I want that, too?"

Bryan's eyes blazed. He crossed his arms over his chest.

Tom pointed his finger at him. "I loved Stephanie, but I didn't treat her right. I wanted a wife, but I didn't want to do any work. And she was too insecure at the time to call me out on it."

"So she went off with another guy."

This time he did flinch. "Yeah. Another guy was smart enough to see what I was too blind and dumb to realize. Stephanie is special. She needed someone to be there for her, to care about her."

"I can't believe I'm listening to this," Bryan shouted, crumpling a napkin and throwing it across the counter. "She cheated on you and you're defending her? I'm staging an intervention."

"She never cheated on me." He ground the words out with deadly conviction.

"Call it what you want, but when a wife lies about where she's at and is caught with another guy, I call it cheating."

"She crossed a line. An emotional line. She admitted it. Yes, I caught her holding hands, but that's as far as it went. She never cheated on me."

"Hope that keeps you warm at night, Tommy." Tom's stomach burned at the hostility pour-

ing down. "I would do anything—anything—
to go back and handle my marriage differently.
But I can't."

"Why would you want to?" Bryan sneered.

"Because I love her!"

Bryan tilted his head as if to say, "See?" and
Tom let out a shaky breath. Sam didn't say a word,
just watched their interaction through wide eyes.

Tom slid his foot along the hardwood floor.
"I never stopped loving her. If I had the slightest chance of creating a new life with her and
Macy, I would, but it's not going to happen. She
doesn't want me."

"She should be so fortunate," Bryan muttered.

That did it. He'd opened up more than ever before, and Bryan kept pushing him. What did his
brother want? Stephanie tied to a stake out front
and lit on fire?

"What is your problem?" Tom asked.

"You're a pushover—that's my problem."

He wanted to punch Bryan—his fists itched
to—but he closed his eyes and stepped backward.
"Get out."

"Glad to."

Stephanie stood on Tom's new porch at eight
o'clock on Valentine's Day. Why she'd driven here
after telling him she had plans, she couldn't say.
After the movie, Bea suggested Macy sleep at
her house, and instead of heading to her apart-

ment, Stephanie had stopped at the video store and zoomed all the way to Lake Endwell. Which was kind of dumb. Maybe he'd asked someone else out. Was he even home?

The door opened. Lackluster eyes and hollow cheeks greeted her. Tom looked haggard.

"Surprise." She opened her hands, lifting her shoulders.

"What are you doing here?" His track pants and gray tee hinted at the hard planes of muscles underneath. "I thought you had plans."

"Um, yeah, so Macy's staying the night at Bea's. Are you busy?" She turned. "Sorry, I should have called."

"Come in." He gestured her inside.

"Are you feeling all right?" She shrugged her coat off and followed him down the hall to the living room. Set her purse next to two empty pizza boxes on the kitchen island.

"Yeah, why?" He padded barefoot to the couch.

"I don't know. You look a little tired."

"Rough day," he called from the other room.

"I'll make you some tea and honey."

"I don't own any tea."

"Well, you must have something." She rummaged through the pantry, not seeing anything suitable for a cold or flu. "What about warm milk?"

"I'm not sick. Come in here. Did you bring a movie?"

She pulled the DVD out of her purse and joined him, careful to sit on the other end of his enormous sectional. "You don't mess around when it comes to big furniture, do you?"

"What? I can't hear you. You're too far away." A grin lit his eyes and he patted the cushion next to him. "I won't bite."

She held back a smile and scooted closer. "Seriously, I think you should go to bed."

He put his hand around her wrist and tugged. "How many times can I tell you? I'm not sick. Now, what movie did you bring? I hope it's nothing too mushy. You know, Valentine's Day and all."

She lifted the cover for him to see. "I don't know, it might get mushy in parts."

He busted out laughing. "*Iron Man?* Really? Brilliant."

The compliment spread through her body. Or maybe it was their proximity. He snatched the movie from her hand and got the DVD player ready, and then he resumed his spot next to her. He smelled good. As if he'd taken a shower.

"You know, you're looking brighter now. Funny what a good movie can do, huh?" She nudged him with her elbow.

"Yeah, this is one of my favorites." His cock-eyed smile slid into something less teasing, more romantic. "Thanks for bringing it over."

"You're welcome." She blinked, smoothing her jeans, anything to keep her hands busy and her gaze elsewhere. How else could she dismiss the sudden yearning pooling in her stomach? "You're sure you don't mind me showing up without Macy?"

"I'm sure."

His breath scorched her neck. When had he gotten so close? And why wasn't he even closer? If she shifted her face a smidge, his lips would be right there.

Stephanie almost jumped up. "Oh, look. It's starting." The copyright message displayed across the screen. And it lingered. For a solid fifteen seconds.

"Is it?" He trailed his finger over the back of her hand. She jumped this time.

"Um, I thought I saw popcorn in there. I'll go make us some." She hurried to the kitchen, her heartbeat thrumming. Why had she come tonight? Her nerves were all over the place, but isn't this what she wanted? So why was she acting like such a twitchy imbecile? It wasn't as if she'd never been kissed.

But this was Tom.

And Tom's kisses left her defenseless. Always had. Always would.

She tore open the plastic seal on the bag of popcorn and pushed the microwave button.

She'd stay on her side of the couch. Yes, sir, she would. The popping built to a crescendo and the machine beeped. Too soon. She wasn't ready to go back in there.

"Want me to start it?" Tom called.

"Yes, be right there." She grabbed the bag, careful to avoid the steam, and returned to the couch. She handed him the popcorn and sat three feet away.

"Don't you want any?" He nodded at the bag. "We can't share with you over in Siberia."

It smelled really good. She inched closer. Took a small handful.

When Tom put his arm around her, she let her cheek fall into his shoulder. It fit just right. Like before. Except this wasn't like before.

"Hold on—this part's intense."

Intense? Yeah. Five years of dormant attraction flooded her at his nearness.

She could get used to this.

But should she?

She snuggled into his embrace. Who cared? She'd enjoy it for the moment. A moment might be all she got.

Chapter Fourteen

Stephanie waved goodbye to Bea as she crossed the parking lot. For once the temperature was above freezing. A fluke for March. Birds even chirped in the air. Maybe she could don one layer of clothing tonight instead of three. It would be great to wear something feminine, something pretty for Parents' Night and not because Tom was joining her.

Well, maybe because Tom was joining her.

Oh, who was she kidding? She hadn't cared about dressing up or doing her hair for any guy but Tom. He'd been the one man to make her stomach flip-flop. The urge may have rested quietly for a few years, but not anymore.

She drove home to get her books and change before class. The past three weeks had made her happier than she'd been in years. Tom had been spending twenty minutes talking to her after his time with Macy. He told her about how the dealerships bounced back from the recession, explained the training involved with the IRONMAN and made her laugh with his insights about life.

She, in turn, showed him the projects she was working on for school, bored him to death with a breakdown of dental insurance woes and made him laugh about Macy's antics.

They'd settled into an easy friendship. The one she'd wanted when married to him.

After skipping up the steps to the apartment building, she almost dropped her keys unlocking her mailbox in the hall. Swiping the bulky stack of mail, she jogged to her apartment, tossed everything on the table and sped to her room. Minutes later she returned, wearing her favorite jeans and a navy T-shirt. She crouched near the dining table to lace her athletic shoes.

The mail caught her eye, but she didn't have time to go through it. Probably a bunch of bills, anyhow. Two manila envelopes were wedged between a catalog and pizza coupons. She finished tying the other shoe, stood and stretched her arms over her head.

Maybe she should call Tom. Remind him about tonight.

She dug through her purse until she found her cell phone. Her finger paused midair.

No.

She'd made it clear she would not be leaving him reminders.

Just because she wanted to hear his voice did not excuse her from playing a role she'd repeatedly told herself she would not play. She had no desire to be the designated cruise director for their co-parenting gig. No one texted *her* about important dates. Either Macy meant enough to him to write it down in the first place or he'd miss the event.

He hadn't let Macy down yet.

But what about all the nights Stephanie had spent alone when they were married? The planned Friday-night movies he hadn't shown up for? The broken promises? Exactly like her mom.

A ripple of hurt slid down Stephanie's spine at all Mom had missed after marrying Jim, husband number two. Stephanie had been eight years old. Mom was in love, again, which meant Stephanie spent her afternoons and evenings with the eighty-year-old lady next door, who slept the entire time. Alone, in front of a television, Stephanie ate a peanut butter sandwich while Mom and Jim enjoyed a honeymoon phase of late nights out. Their honeymoon phase mirrored their dating phase.

Over the years, Stephanie had overheard her dad on the phone reminding Mom about her upcoming dance recital, then her volleyball games, awards nights and on and on. Sometimes Mom came; sometimes she didn't. By the time Stephanie had turned fourteen, it didn't matter anymore. She enjoyed her mom when she bothered to show up, which wasn't often. Stephanie pretended Mom didn't exist the rest of the time. It was easier that way.

The last time Stephanie saw her was after Macy was born. Mom waltzed into Dad's house, tossed one look at the baby and crumpled into a chair, declaring, "I'm too young to be a grandmother."

She'd since married husband number five.

Stephanie stared at her purse and teetered between the past and the present. Tom wasn't like her mother. He'd be there tonight. She'd emailed him the details last week, and the preschool had sent them both postcards.

Hitching her backpack onto her shoulder, her gaze fell on the pile of mail again, and she quickly sorted through it.

One of the manila envelopes held her health insurance resource book. The other was from the University of Miami. She ripped it open.

Sliding the cover letter out, she scanned it.

We're pleased to...

She did it! She was accepted!

She skimmed the rest, her heart tripping overtime at the second-to-last paragraph.

A scholarship. Not for the full amount, but it would cover some of her tuition. Her money problems were disappearing before her eyes.

Hugging the packet to her chest, she closed her eyes and imagined it all. The beach, the turquoise water, the sun beating down on her and Macy as they held hands and raced into the waves. Dad's condo with its loft for Macy and an extra bedroom for her. Dad. Always providing for her. Always there for her.

A new life. A better life.

But…a life without Tom.

Her spirits fell.

When had he become so important to her? Just the thought of Miami made her feel as if she was ditching her best friend.

Maybe she was.

She flung the manila envelope onto the coffee table and raced out of the apartment. She'd have to think about it later. She was late.

At mile fifteen, Tom jogged the hill leading to the park. He'd skipped out of the dealership early when he realized the thermometer read fifty degrees. Calls and invoices could wait. The sun, blue sky and clean air made it the perfect day for a long run outside. Even robins flew back and forth overhead in excitement, a sure sign winter was almost over. The only other sound was the *slap, slap* of his shoes hitting the pavement.

Monday night, he'd bought a bike attachment for Macy to pedal behind his when the weather got nicer. He wouldn't be able to ride as fast or as far as he would solo, but any bike time was better than none. Plus, he wanted her to enjoy being active outdoors the way he had as a kid.

At the top of the hill, he slowed a moment to appreciate the glimmer of the lake in the distance. In less than two months this view would come alive with pink apple blossoms, yellow daffodils and red tulips. Spring in Lake Endwell was almost as nice as fall.

Checking his watch, he calculated how much time he had. Enough to finish his run, take a shower and drive to Macy's preschool. He had no idea what they did at Parents' Night, but he'd soon find out. Pride filled his chest. Being a dad never got old.

For the rest of the run, he mentally went over upcoming tasks at work and the groceries he needed to pick up later. He'd forgotten to call Claire. She kept insisting on throwing him a housewarming party, but the family had been so busy, they hadn't been able to set a date.

He made the first turn into his subdivision. Next Saturday would work. He slowed to a walk to cool down. Bryan stood on his porch.

"Haven't seen you in a few weeks." He brushed past Bryan and let them in through the front door. "Have a seat while I grab a Gatorade. You want anything?"

Bryan shook his head, continued through the foyer to the back of the house and sat at the table. Tom chugged the orange drink and joined him.

"I've been thinking a lot." Bryan's dull eyes were downright depressing. "Talked to Claire."

Tom wanted to reply. To joke and say something like, "Well, that's your problem right there," but too much time had passed since he'd thrown Bryan out and too many things had been said that night.

"You were right—I've been a jerk. And it wasn't about you." Bryan thumped his knuckles on the table and peered out the window. "I give you credit. You really shook up your life and changed it, didn't you?"

"I'm still me. Still here. The same old brother you've always had."

A hint of a smile crossed Bryan's lips. "You moved on. And I'm jealous. I didn't know that when I yelled at you, but…"

"Claire?"

"Yeah. She helped me see it. Asked me all kinds of Claire-questions. You know, about how my life has changed since you moved out."

Tom had been busy thinking of his own life,

wants and dreams. He hadn't given much thought to how it would affect Bryan. "Is living with Sam so bad?"

"No," Bryan said with a laugh. "I'm getting to know him better. He's not such a pest now he's grown up."

A pang of longing hit Tom—for the past, for camaraderie he only had when he was with Bryan. They'd been best friends their whole lives. Knew each other better than anyone.

Well, except Stephanie. The past month had drawn Tom closer to her. Close enough to understand her, respect her, to know her.

"I've got to do something," Bryan said. "You know how you said you were just sitting there these years? Well, at least you found a goal. I think I've wasted my life since my divorce. I have nothing to show for it and no idea how to fix it." Bryan opened his palms. "I can't spend the rest of my life like this."

Tom understood. He'd sunk to his lowest point at the end of last summer. "I know. I get it. I'd been coasting along fine until one day last August. I was in Granddad's fishing boat and I looked up. Saw his cottage perched up there, just like I'd seen it a million times before. And I snapped. I couldn't take another minute of the same old, same old. That's when I started researching the IRONMAN. Signed up that night."

"But I don't want to compete in a triathlon. I have no idea what I want to do."

"You'll find your own way to get out of the slump. What do you like? What have you always wanted to do?"

"I don't know." Bryan's eyes shimmered a moment, then dimmed. "I just don't know."

"You always liked baseball. Why don't you join an adult league?"

He made a sour face. "I'm not twelve anymore."

"Coach a team, then." Tom put his hand on Bryan's shoulder. "You'll figure it out."

"Maybe I should haul out Granddad's fishing boat. Lightning might strike twice." Bryan held his gaze. "I'm sorry for all the stuff I said about Stephanie. If you think you can trust her, then go for it."

Trust. Something he used to believe he'd never be able to do again where Stephanie was concerned.

"I needed to blame her," Tom said. "It helped me cope."

Bryan hesitated. "Why don't you blame her anymore? What changed?"

"When I look back, I see the ways she tried to reach me." He met Bryan's gaze. "You know the day I saw her walking around the park with that guy? She wasn't smiling or laughing. She was miserable. Even with him."

"Maybe she's an unhappy person. Maybe nothing and no one will make her happy."

The view from the window showed the dead grass, dark green pines and gray branches. Dormant before spring. He knew the feeling.

"I don't think so, Bryan. I think we both changed."

The faint ticking of the kitchen clock filled the room.

"Tommy?"

He turned his attention back to Bryan. "Hmm?"

"Are you really willing to risk it again?"

That was the question. He'd been flipping it over for weeks.

Was he willing to risk his heart on her again? Without any guarantees this time would be different? She'd given him a few hints she was interested, like stopping by on Valentine's Day. If he offered her a place in his life, would she take it for herself or for security? He didn't want a future without love, without passion.

"I don't know," Tom said.

Bryan lifted one shoulder. "At least she's being mature about Macy."

Macy! "I'm late for Macy's open house. I've got to take a quick shower and get out of here. I'll call you when it's over."

Bryan stood. "That's okay, man. We can talk another time. You'd better hurry. Your kid's special."

"You can say that again." He grinned. His kid was special.

"Where's Daddy?" Macy craned her neck while tugging on Stephanie's sleeve. "Where is he?"

Stephanie put her serene mask on as her gut churned. *Don't do this to her, Tom. Don't get her hopes up if you're going to let her down.* "I don't know. Maybe he's running late."

He'd better get there. She clutched her purse to her side. The pain of being an afterthought never went away. Shouldn't a parent put their kid first? She was certainly trying her best to do just that with Macy, and here it was, the first mutual parent event, and Tom hadn't arrived.

"Why don't you go say hi to Tatum?" Stephanie pointed to the wall where Tatum and her parents stood. Her mom held a baby wrapped in a blue blanket. A stab of pain pierced Stephanie's heart.

A baby.

Two kids. And a husband. A family.

"I don't want to see Tatum. I want Daddy."

Stephanie closed her eyes a moment. The uncertainty, the bravado and the desperation in

Macy's tone reminded her all too much of her own hours waiting on Mom. The nervous watching of the door. The minutes ticking down. The desire to show her friends she had a mom who cared just as they did.

"Hi, Macy!" Tatum ran over, hugging Macy and spinning her. "You wanna go see my brother?"

Stephanie bent and smiled. "Hi, Tatum. What's your brother's name?"

"That's Jaden." Tatum grabbed Macy's hand. "Let's go see him and get cookies!"

Stephanie watched them run away as she reached for her phone.

Don't do it. Stay strong.

"Hi, Stephanie."

Uh-oh. She tried to hide her annoyance as Robert, single dad to Max, neared. He stood a little too close. He always stood a little too close. She inched away. "Hi, Robert."

"How are your classes going? If I remember correctly, you're almost done."

She exhaled. He was a nice guy. Tall, on the gangly side, but with dark blond hair, amber eyes and a ready smile. The other single moms loved him, but she kept her distance, or tried to anyway. "I'll be finished the end of April. Then I'm off to grad school."

"Off?" He frowned, leaning in until she could

see the faint nick on his cheek from shaving. "Don't tell me you're moving?"

Maybe he had personal-space issues. He didn't seem to understand the proper boundary. She backed up a step. Into a chest. A rock-hard one at that.

"Oof! I'm sorry." She turned, looking up into Tom's sharp face.

"Well?" The gleam in Tom's eyes sparked her indignation. "Are you?"

"What are you talking about?" Who was he to show up late and skewer her with his gorgeous blue eyes?

"Moving. Are you moving?" A hard edge glinted in his tone. He put his hand on her arm. Possessive.

She stiffened and shifted away from him. "I'm not sure what my plans are yet."

Robert narrowed his eyes at Tom but extended his hand. "Robert. Max's dad."

"Thomas Sheffield. Macy's dad." He shook Robert's hand. Neither appeared pleased.

Did Tom think she was flirting with Robert? She drew her lips together. If he did, who cared? She had nothing to be ashamed of. Not this time anyway.

"I'll let Macy know you're here." She leveled a stare his way. "She's been waiting."

He opened his mouth to reply, but she spun on her heel and searched for Macy.

Adrenaline mounted with each step. He had no right to be angry. If anyone did, it was her. Sneaking up like that. Giving her the look. Interrupting her conversation. Working out all the time and having a superfit body. Should be a crime.

She spotted Macy in a corner with a group of girls. "Macy, your dad's here."

"He is?" Macy's face lit, and she sprinted into Tom's arms.

Naturally, he picked her up and kissed her. Like some sort of hero. She snorted. Easy to be a hero when you could show up whenever you wanted. And it wasn't as if he'd had to wrangle the brush through Macy's hair or wash her face or squeeze her legs into tights all while trying to whip up a box of mac and cheese. He had it easy, that man did.

Adjusting her features out of irritation mode, Stephanie resumed her spot between Tom and Robert. They were discussing the latest case Robert worked on as a corporate law attorney. After a few minutes, she cleared her throat. Robert instantly closed the gap between them. "Is your throat dry? I'll get you some punch."

"Macy," Tom said. "Aren't you going to introduce me to your teachers?"

"Yes, Daddy." She dragged him over to two teachers by the desk.

Near the refreshment table, Stephanie listened with half an ear to what Robert was blathering on about, but she kept Tom in her sights. It didn't escape her notice that most of the women there kept Tom in their sights, too.

She sighed. He was too handsome. The poor man didn't even realize it. The teachers he chatted with practically fluttered when he spoke. They might need nerve medication after tonight.

"So what do you say? Should we get the kids together for a playdate while you and I catch up over coffee?" Robert was saying. The invitation in his eye warned her a playdate wasn't all he was after.

"I'm pretty busy with school and all. Oh, there's Jen—could you excuse me?" She sidled up to a group of moms and introduced herself to a straggler. The interaction was over before it began. Robert glued himself to her side.

When did this open house end? If she had to spend even five more minutes watching women fawn all over Tom while she tried to avoid Robert, she was going to flip out.

The rock star of Parents' Night himself stood between two of Macy's teachers. One of them cackled at something Tom said. "We are delighted you came tonight, Mr. Sheffield."

Delighted? My word. She'd have to find the smelling salts for those ladies soon.

"Call me Tom. Everyone does."

Giggling ensued. "Okay, Tom."

Giggling? Stephanie squinted. Was the woman blushing?

"And don't be a stranger. We love Macy. Such a bright and sweet little girl."

That did it. She marched to the hooks where she'd hung her and Macy's coats. Tom couldn't help he was gorgeous. He'd been friendly and everything he should be. So what really bothered her?

The female attention?

No.

If she was brutally honest with herself, she resented his get-out-of-jail-free card in showing up late. No one seemed to mind. Not Macy. Not the teachers.

Just her.

"Not leaving so soon, are you?" Robert touched her hand. She jumped.

"Oh, ah, it's getting late." She waited for him to move aside, but he didn't budge.

"Late?" He laughed. "It's early. Stay."

"Hey, Steph?" Tom appeared at her side. "Do you mind if I come over?"

Yes, she minded. Everything about Tom lit her

nerves like a bonfire tonight, but creepy Robert didn't have to know that. "Suit yourself."

Tom stood there a minute, then led her outside the classroom to the empty hallway. "What's going on?"

"Nothing." She adjusted the sleeves of her jacket and refused to look at him.

"Could have fooled me."

"I'm mad, okay? Do you have any idea how worried Macy was that you wouldn't come?"

"I'm here now."

"Well, good for you."

Robert wandered into the hallway. The muscle in Tom's cheek throbbed. "This isn't a good place to discuss this. I'll follow you home."

Stephanie nodded, then hurried to the bathroom, locking the door behind her. What was her problem? Tom was here. Macy was happy. So why did she feel like crying?

She stared into the mirror and saw herself as a young girl. Felt the bullets in her heart from all the times her mom let her down.

God, my heart still breaks for the little girl I was, and it's never going to change. Mom will never be a real mother to me.

Stephanie turned the faucet on and splashed cold water on her cheeks. She straightened.

One thing she had now that she didn't have then was a heavenly Father. One who wiped away her tears. One who would never let her down. But a part of her still hurt. A part of her would always hurt for her broken childhood.

Chapter Fifteen

Tom draped his coat on the back of Stephanie's dining chair. From the bathroom, Macy belted out a tune about a rainbow and lollipops. Stephanie barely made eye contact. "I'm sorry I was late to the open house," he said.

"I need to finish getting Macy ready for bed." Stephanie's rigid back disappeared down the hall.

He'd messed up. Earlier, when he'd arrived at the preschool, his lungs had seized at the sight of that Robert character. The guy had drooled all over Steph, clearly ignoring her get-lost signals. What Tom wouldn't have done to drag his sorry excuse of a body out into the hall and explain the lady needed some space. But he'd had to stand there and grit his teeth because he had no right when it came to Stephanie.

No right.

And he wanted that right.

Macy, in a Disney princess nightgown, ran into the living room. "Can we read a bedtime story, Daddy? Please?" She hopped onto his lap and pressed his cheeks between her palms. "Pretty please?"

He stood, lifting her high in the air. "If it's okay with your mom."

"Can we, Mommy?" Macy shouted.

"Just one," Stephanie yelled from the hall. "A short one."

"Yay!"

Tom carried her to her room and let her select a book, something about a kitten in the snow. After tucking her in, he sat on the bed and read. Then he kissed Macy's forehead, said a prayer and went back into the living room, where Stephanie sipped hot tea.

"Like I said, I'm sorry I was late."

"Okay." Her posture and tone assured him it was not okay.

"Bryan stopped by. He and I have been having some problems lately."

She set her mug on the end table. "Let me guess. About me, right?"

He averted his gaze. This wasn't going as planned. Well, he didn't have a plan. Why had he come over? "Not really. We're both at an odd place in life. It's hard to explain."

"What's hard to explain about it? You're fitting your daughter into your life, and you're stuck dealing with me again. It's not that complicated."

"I don't consider myself stuck."

"But Bryan does, doesn't he? He can't understand why you're nice to me. Not after all I put you through. Nailed it, didn't I?" She let out a joyless laugh. "Face it, Tom. Your family will never accept me. Not after the mistakes I made."

"They already accept you." He wanted to believe it.

"Libby does? Bryan? Sure, Tom. If it keeps you warm at night, keep living in fantasyland." She grabbed the tea again.

Her mood confused him. Angry, hurt and bitter—but why? He hadn't seen her like this…ever. Not even when they were married.

"What's going on, Steph? You're upset. What happened?"

"Macy worried you weren't coming. And what could I say? I had no idea if you were or not. Do you know how many times my mother didn't show up for me? How many times you didn't? If you're not going to come, don't say you will."

"I did come. I wanted to come. I got held up."

"You could have let me know."

True. "You're right. I should have texted you."

Neither spoke for a while. Loud clunks in the hall outside faded. The neighbors must have returned.

"Did you think I was flirting with Robert?" Her stricken eyes met his.

Taken aback, he shook his head. "No. He was all over you. He's due for a lesson on reading a woman's signals. Or a shot of pepper spray."

A smile flitted over her lips.

Tom rested his elbows on his knees and leaned forward. "You don't need permission to go out with Robert if you want to. You don't owe me anything, you know."

"I see," she murmured.

"I wish—" He pushed off the couch and stood, rubbing his chin. The University of Miami packet on the coffee table caught his attention. He frowned as he picked up the letter, casting a questioning stare at Stephanie. "May I?"

Her face paled, but she nodded, her chin high.

Scanning the sheet, he held it for a moment, then let it flutter back to the table. He sat back on the couch. "You were accepted. And a scholarship." His voice sounded normal, but inside he warred between what he wanted and what she needed. "What about Western?"

She crossed one leg over the other. "I applied. Haven't heard back yet."

"No?" He swallowed, unsure of his next move.

Wanted to haul her into his arms and demand she stay. Admit to her he loved her. Ask her for another chance. Bribe her with his big house. But instead he prayed.

Lord, I love this woman. I do. But all I can offer is here, and she wants to be somewhere else.

"It's a good deal." He pointed to the letter. His heart cracked, but he had to see this through. "Do you think you'd be happy in Florida?"

She smiled, and the tension in her face disappeared, leaving her younger, carefree. "I don't know. I like to think I would."

That smile—that hopeful, forward-looking reaction—convinced him. "I want you to be happy. Don't stay here for me or out of guilt. I'll fly down as often as I can to see Macy. We'll make it work."

Her cheeks caved in, and her eyes dulled. "What do you mean? You don't want me to stay?"

"Of course I want you to stay." He speared his hand through his hair. "The thought of not seeing Macy is tearing me up. I want to see her every day."

"Macy." She stood up, held one wrist with her other hand.

He faced her, aching to take her in his arms. "And you. Maybe you don't feel it. I don't know, but I feel it." He moved closer, ran the back of his hand gently over her hair. "You're special. Beautiful."

Her lips parted slightly, and she moved closer to his hand. "I feel it." The words were husky. She stayed near him.

"Do you think about it—us, together again?" Inches separated them. He lowered his chin to claim her gaze. "A family."

"Yes," she whispered.

He couldn't look away from her lips. "I would do things differently this time."

"Me, too."

He caressed her cheek, leaning forward and brushing her lips with his. Soft. So soft. Wrapping one arm around her waist, he pulled her close. His other hand crept behind her neck, fingers sliding through her silky hair, to explore the kiss. All the pent-up emotion from the past months bubbled to the surface, but he controlled it, not wanting to frighten her. Instead he poured every ounce of tenderness into his actions. Her sweetness floored him. Made his muscles tense, made him want to protect her.

Then her arms glided over his shoulders, and everything changed. He wanted to give himself, his life, his future to her. Wanted to present himself as an offering.

Slowly, he ended the kiss. His heart thumped

over and over. He searched her eyes, recognizing fear and confusion mingled with hope.

"I'd give you everything, you know," he said, his voice raw.

She blinked. "You already have."

The wistfulness didn't cover the resignation in her voice. Tom stilled, not knowing what to make of her. Did she mean he gave her everything the first go-round and it wasn't enough? Was his best, his everything, not enough for her?

She ran her hand up and down her arm. "You have such a big heart. I want to, but—no, I can't. I can't do this to you."

"Do what to me?" Tom's cheekbones strained against his skin.

Stephanie cringed. Her words had come out all wrong. If she could take them back, she would. "Forget it."

"What did you mean?"

"It's hard to put into words."

"Try me."

She lifted her eyes to the ceiling, trying to formulate her thoughts. The Tom she'd married had been self-centered but loyal. This Tom—the mature man in front of her—took her breath away. So he'd been a little late to the event tonight. He'd made it *and* showed Macy how important she was to him by coming home and tucking her into bed.

This man would willingly give her, Stephanie, another chance.

His kiss—so generous, so mind-blowing—said he wanted her. But what if his real attraction was the idea of a family? To be together for Macy?

Stephanie wrung her fingers together. "It's a big risk, toying with forever again."

"No clue what you're talking about." His legs had widened warrior-style, and he crossed his arms.

She sighed, opened her hands. "Take Macy out of the equation. Would we be having this conversation?"

"It's not relevant." He dismissed her words with a wave.

"It is."

"We wouldn't have crossed paths."

"No, but—" She tucked her hair behind her ear. "We're in a unique situation. I don't want to trap you with our daughter. I don't want you waking up in two years resenting me."

"But what if I want our daughter? What if I want you and me and her together?"

"I can't ruin your life again."

He closed the distance between them, holding her biceps in his hands. "You wouldn't. I've changed. You've changed."

"I know you've changed. But me? I'm scared."

She broke free, rubbing her arms. "What if I hurt you?"

"Is that what this is about?" He straightened. "I'm still not enough for you, am I?"

"You've always been enough for me." She jabbed her finger into her chest, emotion rising. "I'm the one who's not enough for you. Or for anyone. Why can't you see it?"

"What are you saying? No matter who you're with, you wouldn't be enough? What does that mean?"

"I don't know!"

"Then what? Why are you blowing me off?"

How could she put in words what she didn't understand? This wasn't about blowing him off. "I couldn't live with myself if I screwed up again."

"So you don't want to try. Got it." Neither broke eye contact until finally his jaw shifted. He grabbed his coat and stalked out, slamming the door behind him.

She didn't move at first. The evening came into sharp focus but blurred when she tried to hold on to a moment. Maybe they were both right *and* wrong. When they were married, she'd wanted him home. And she clearly hadn't been enough to keep him by her side or he would have made more of an effort.

And now? They'd grown up. Their mistakes wouldn't necessarily be repeated. Not if they both tried harder. He acted as if he loved her, as if he wanted them to be a couple again. But he kept mentioning Macy and being a family. The nagging voice in her brain kept whining Macy came first, and Stephanie only got thrown in as part of the package.

After locking the door, she spun and headed to the kitchen. Filled the sink with soapy water. Tom's kiss kept coming back, overloading her senses. His kiss was more than physical. He'd poured his soul into it, and she drank it up, remembering how magnificent it had been when she was his.

Addictive. Being his, being Tom's. She'd been special when they first started dating. He'd made her feel like something precious.

She admired him then. She admired him now.

Thrusting the dirty dishes into the sink, she methodically washed the first glass. What would it be like to be with Tom again, now, with Macy? To walk down the aisle. To move into that big, beautiful house. To have support—his support all day, every day. To go to church as a family.

To have more babies who looked like Tom.

She dropped the glass into the water and put her hand over her mouth, suds dripping onto the floor.

Why was she doing this? *Stupid, stupid, stupid.* She couldn't afford to indulge in these what-ifs. She picked up the glass, the warm water seeping through her fingers.

His kiss. His love. His appreciation.

She wanted it. Oh, how she wanted it.

Carefully, she rinsed the glass and placed it upside down on the dish towel, let out a shaky breath and stared unseeing at the wall, her head moving back and forth as if to shut out the thought.

Had she ever *not* been in love with him?

Head spinning, she fought the dizziness threatening to send her to the floor.

She'd always loved him.

Would always love him.

The urge to pray, to ask for guidance, rained down hard on her soul, but she resisted. What if God told her to do the impossible? How could she move to Florida if her heart was here? And how could she stay in Michigan and risk it all for a man who might only have strong feelings for the mother of his child?

She'd been right to warn Tom. Not the way he understood it—who knew what went through his mind?—but she needed more. She didn't want to be loved for being Macy's mom. She wanted to be cherished for being herself. And she hadn't been enough to keep him home, to keep him interested in her before. She could try, she could give him every ounce of love she had, but somehow she would still let him down.

Closing her eyes, she exhaled. She just had to stay strong.

* * *

"Are you busy?" From his driveway, Tom called Claire on his cell phone. He couldn't bring himself to walk into his huge empty house. Not now. Not after Stephanie had flat out told him she thought she'd ruin his life. Didn't take a genius to figure out his feelings for her ran way deeper than her feelings for him did. At least this time she'd been honest about it.

"No, Reed went over to his dad's for a while. Why?"

"Mind if I come over?"

"Of course not. The door's open. Come in when you get here."

He hung up and backed out of his drive. A full moon lit the sky, and he flicked the radio on to a country station, changing the channel at the girl-done-me-wrong song. As if he wanted to hear that. He kept flipping channels. Commercial. Commercial. A rapper boasting about clubs and money. Another commercial. Celine Dion. He paused. Stephanie's smiling face popped into his mind. He pulled into Claire's drive.

This was bad.

He was listening to Celine Dion.

And he knew the words. They were even starting to make sense.

He got out of the truck, slammed the door and

jogged to Claire's front porch, knocking twice and letting himself in.

With a big grin, she waved from the sectional sofa. "Hey, it's good to see you."

He didn't return the smile but tore off his coat and tossed it on the closet handle before joining her.

"What happened?" She faced him, concern in her eyes.

Where to start? Maybe he should go home. Face the empty house. It would be easier than trying to figure out what had happened tonight.

She scooted forward and sauntered to the kitchen. "You need ice cream."

"I'm a guy, Claire. We don't drown our problems in ice cream."

Peeking around the corner, she held up half a gallon. "You're not hungry?"

"What flavor is it?" Ice cream sounded kind of good.

"Mint chocolate chip."

"Fine."

Two minutes later she handed him a heaping bowl of ice cream with rivers of chocolate syrup drizzled on top. She carried her bowl to the corner of the couch and propped her knees up. "So what's going on?"

He licked the spoon. "Steph might be moving to Miami."

"Right. The master's degree."

"But I asked her to consider staying. To go to Western like she is now."

"Sure. Makes sense. That way you can still see Macy." She took another bite and thought a moment. "She's moving to Miami, isn't she?"

A knock on the door startled them. He craned his neck back to see who it was. Libby stepped inside, smiling when she noticed him. Inwardly, he groaned. Claire was a good listener. She could usually see angles to a situation he couldn't, and she gave balanced advice. Libby, on the other hand, blurted out whatever was on her mind. It rarely helped.

"Fancy meeting you here." She shimmied out of her coat and wedged herself between them. "How've you been? Enjoying your new house?"

He shoveled in another bite of ice cream and shrugged. Better to keep his mouth shut. He was confused enough. He didn't need Libby muddying the waters more.

"Don't tell me you're sick of it already," Libby said. "We're planning your housewarming party for Saturday. I even invited Stephanie."

"You did?"

She chuckled. "Yeah. I did."

"Why?"

She picked at her pink nail polish. "Figured you'd want me to. Anyway, she's not so bad."

"What brought about this change of heart?"

Libby and Claire exchanged glances. Then Libby patted his hand. "It's okay. We know you've been spending a lot of time with her—"

"What are you talking about?"

"You skipped the Christmas church service with us, gave her a special tour of your house before any of us saw it, and you run off to see Macy every spare minute. I assumed you were considering getting back together."

"I was." Why did he admit that? "But not now."

"Why?" Libby asked.

Claire unfolded her legs. "Stephanie is moving to Miami."

Tom straightened. "I didn't say that."

"She's not?" Claire sounded surprised.

"I don't know. I've got to go." He set the half-eaten bowl on the end table and started to rise.

"Sit!" Libby and Claire said in unison. He glared at them, then sank back into the cushions. "Tell us what is going on."

"I want Stephanie to stay, but I also want her to be happy."

"What's so special about Miami?" Libby didn't sound sarcastic, just curious.

He considered. "Well, for one, her dad is there. I know she's wanted to go since he moved last year. Other than that, I'm not sure."

"Haven't you asked her?" Claire gave him a look assuring him he was stupid.

"No, I didn't ask her," he snapped. Why hadn't he asked her?

"Yeah, why would he, Claire? He wants her here. If he reminds her of all the reasons she's set on Miami, he'll run her off." Libby tossed her blond hair as if the concept was ludicrous.

"Exactly." Maybe his baby sister wasn't so bad to talk to after all.

Claire rolled her eyes, then gave them her patient stare. "Okay, what's keeping her here?"

"Duh." Libby jerked her thumb his way. "Tommy."

"Tommy, the father of Macy? Her ex-husband? Or the man she loves?"

"She doesn't love me." The words sprinted from his mouth.

"How do you know?" Libby asked.

"I just left her place, and we weren't throwing out words like *love*, but she made it clear we don't have a future together."

Claire muttered, "As if the world would stop turning if you mention love. Men."

Libby narrowed her eyes at him. "Do you love her?"

He clamped his mouth shut and fixed his gaze on the television.

"You do." Libby nodded to Claire. "He does."

Claire leaned forward. "Does she know you love her, Tommy?"

"Well, I didn't say it in so many words, but she should know."

"Should know?" Libby threw her hands up. "Given the history of you two, I'd think you'd want to spell everything out and not leave it up to her to decipher. Haven't you had enough misunderstandings?"

"I'm scared, okay," he blurted out. Stupid sisters. They could tear a confession out of a terrorist. "She left me. I wasn't enough. And I'm still not."

"What?" Libby's outrage came through loud and clear. "Did she say that?"

"No!"

"What exactly did she say?" Claire asked gently.

"She told me I wanted her for the wrong reasons. That she'd hurt me again."

"What in the world did she mean by that?" Libby's face screwed up.

Claire held out a hand. "Tommy, did you make it clear to her you aren't trying to get back together just for Macy's sake?"

"What is it with you and her, blaming my feelings on Macy? Of course I want to be a family. I can't leave Macy out of it."

A commercial blared through the television.

"I wouldn't take you, either." Libby hitched her chin in the air. "If we were together—take the whole sibling thing out of the equation, gross— and you wanted me back for our daughter's sake, I'd turn you down flat."

"But that's not what I want—"

Claire bit her lower lip. "Then spell it out for Stephanie."

"She doesn't want me."

"Are you sure she even knows you want her? Do you really know what you want, Tommy?"

"Yeah. I want to get out of here." He lurched to his feet, grabbed his coat and stormed to the door.

"Don't go." Claire stood.

"Stay," Libby said from the couch.

"I can't." He cast one more glance at their faces—full of empathy—and shook his head. Then he marched out and got back into his truck. As he drove, all the things they said pounded him.

Had he made it clear to Stephanie he wanted her? She kept bringing the conversation back to Macy, but he never intended her to think all he was after was a family. So he'd been honest about not reconnecting if Macy wasn't a factor. Macy *was* a factor, and his sisters and Stephanie could act as if she wasn't, but it didn't change the facts. What did they want from him, anyhow?

His truck ate up the miles between Claire's house and his. He trotted up the porch and through the door. Kicked off his shoes and threw his body on the couch. The silence surrounded him, engulfed him, made him feel small and alone.

I'm miserable, God. Why can't this be easy? Why can't she stay here? With me?

He dropped his head in his hands. What if Stephanie did move to Florida?

No more Macy. No more horsey rides and Bible stories and giggles and hugs.

His sisters thought he wanted Stephanie back only so he could be with Macy. What did they know?

He squeezed his eyes shut.

Would he miss Stephanie as much as Macy?

He pictured Stephanie with her brown eyes twinkling, her patience with Macy, her big smile, the dark circles under her eyes when she studied too hard. The sacrifices she'd made and continued to make. She'd changed. The sweet girl he'd fallen in love with back then had become a strong, courageous woman even more beautiful than before.

Yes. His chest tightened. Eyes burned. He'd miss Stephanie.

As much as Macy. Maybe more.

God, why did You let me go and do such a stupid thing? I didn't want to fall in love with her again. And here I am, worse off than the first time.

He fell back against the couch cushions. If he knew how it would all turn out, he'd know how to go forward. What if he did what Claire suggested and laid his heart out for Stephanie? Told her in no uncertain terms that, yes, he loved her and wanted her to stay. He wanted them to be a family.

Would she turn him down? Move to Florida?

He jumped up and paced the room. Grabbed his tattered Bible from the office and leafed through until he found the psalm he'd read a thousand times over the past five years. *"How long must I wrestle with my thoughts and day after day have sorrow in my heart?"*

Forever? No. God didn't work like that. Why would He send His Son to die for everyone if He wanted everyone to be miserable? He wouldn't.

You'll work this out for my good, won't You?

Stephanie and Macy moving to Florida could not be God's plan. But what if…it was?

Then he'd deal with it. He'd be alone again. Training for a race that was infinitely less important than Stephanie or Macy were. Loneliness settled on him.

You're enough.

He blinked. Where had that thought come from?

You've always been enough.

And for once, he believed it.

Chapter Sixteen

"Tom's sister invited me to his housewarming party." Stephanie typed a patient's information into the computer and glanced over at Bea, who was sitting at the other computer station.

"The nice sister or the one who hates you?"

"Believe it or not, Libby sent it. The hater."

"Maybe the nice one made her." Bea slid a stack of papers into a folder. "Or Tom could have insisted."

"No, I don't think so. She included a note. It was pretty decent of her."

"Why don't you think Tom asked her to send it?" Bea got up, filed the folder and scanned the shelf for the next one. When she found it, she plunked it on the desk.

"Haven't seen or talked to him since Wednesday night."

"So? Two days go by. Whoop-dee-doo."

The office had emptied, since they were getting ready to close, but Stephanie leaned over anyway and in a hushed tone said, "We kissed."

Bea slowly spun in her chair, raised her eyebrows, then scooted closer. "Well. Now we're talking. What kind of kiss? The old peck on the cheek or va-va-va-voom?"

Heat rose to her face. Was she really talking to Bea about kissing? She hadn't acted this dippy as a teenager. "The latter."

Bea rubbed her hands together, her eyes shooting rainbows and stars. "Does this mean what I'm hoping?"

"What are you hoping?" Stephanie cast her a sideways glance and resumed typing in the information.

"Don't play coy with me. I don't think you ever got over him. And now look who's back. Kissing and everything."

"It was a mistake. I should never have let him kiss me. We're not getting back together."

"Mmm-hmm." Bea continued filing the stack of papers next to her.

"He loves Macy—there's no question about that—but I'm kind of part of the package, you know. I want to be more than Macy's mom."

"Hold on. Do you think he's using you?"

She considered. "No. Definitely not. I think

he likes the idea of being a family, but it's more for Macy."

Bea seemed to see right through her.

Stephanie threw her hands up. "What? Why are you looking at me like that?"

"Let's back up a minute. What gives you that impression?"

"He doesn't deny he wants to spend more time with Macy. And he's never pretended he wants me to move to Florida." Although, now she thought about it, the other night he had mentioned her taking the scholarship. Said he would make it work. He'd been kind, standing there in his dress shirt and tie. Looking like every woman's dream. Looking like *her* dream.

Bea lifted a finger. "You're not helping your case."

"Maybe he got caught up in memories. In the moment. I don't know."

"Or maybe he loves you and wants another chance."

She gulped and tried to focus on the patient form. He did act like it. His intense blue eyes had drilled into her.

"Stephanie? Are you sure Tom is the issue here?"

"What do you mean?"

"You're inferring all these motives in his actions, but there doesn't seem to be much basis for them. What happened when you were married that has you so scared to take another chance on him?"

Stephanie whirled to face her. "I told you. I made a lot of bad choices."

"Okay, fine, but you're older now. I know you. You've got buckets of integrity. Maybe you didn't like yourself back then, but why don't you now?"

"I like myself." She flipped the patient form over with a *whoosh*. "Of course I like myself."

"Then why are you so sure Tom doesn't?"

She held her breath. The clock on the wall ticked the seconds off. She wasn't sure. Not at all. And she needed him to not like her. Because if he didn't...

Bea tapped the folder on the desk. "Before you write him off, you might want to consider the possibility he loves you. You. Not just Macy."

Stephanie shifted her jaw. "Look, I love happily-ever-afters as much as the next person, but not everyone gets them."

"Not everyone is brave enough to go after them. You are. I believe in you, Stephanie." Bea crossed to the wall of files again.

Her throat swelled. Bea believed in her? She almost asked why. And the thought stopped her short. Why should Bea believing in her be hard to fathom? And why was she so certain Tom didn't love her?

He hadn't said it. He'd hinted. His smoldering, honest gaze had assured her he still had feelings. But how deep did they go? And would they last? Forever? And what if they didn't and her heart ached for more? Would she hurt him? Again?

Her head dipped into her hands. *Lord, I think Bea might be right. I am scared to take another chance on him. Not just for me. But for his sake. I'm not perfect—You know that. How can I be selfish enough to take what he's offering?*

What was he offering? They hadn't discussed love or marriage. Just a blip down memory lane and a few what-if questions. Hardly a basis to get so worked up over. Time to put the whole situation out of her mind. Nothing would come of it, anyhow. Not unless...

Lead me to Your will, Lord. Guide me and make my path straight.

She hoped a straight path meant the safe one. The one where her heart remained intact. The one where she didn't have to worry Tom would tire of her and she'd leave him a casualty again. The highway to Florida was her best option.

Stroke. Breathe. Stroke. Breathe. Tom sliced through the water at the Y. Almost finished with his laps, and he was no closer to a decision than before. He'd shuffled about like a walking dead man the past two days. His sisters called and left text messages, but he ignored them both. Bryan had stopped by. They watched an action movie and kept the conversation to small talk. That's why he loved his brother. He wasn't prying and prodding and making suggestions like Claire or Libby.

Tom reached the wall, flipped under and pushed off the way Sean had trained him, dolphin kicking his legs together until he burst through the surface and continued swimming.

Out of all the women Tom could have dated and fallen in love with, why did he have to go and fall for the one who didn't want him?

He pictured her velvety eyes after they kissed. She wanted him. But she wouldn't admit it. Talked in riddles. Put up walls.

And why was that?

Who knew?

Stroke. Breathe. Stroke. Breathe.

He was tired of analyzing. If she wanted to leave, let her leave. She'd taken his heart last time and he'd survived.

But his heart had grown bigger. His heart wasn't only in Steph's hands. It was in Macy's, too.

He touched the edge and stopped swimming. Resting his arm on the side of the pool, he took a few seconds to let his heart rate return to normal.

"Hey, Tom," Sean called from the door and

sauntered toward him. "Just the man I wanted to see."

Tom flipped his goggles to the top of his head. "How's it going?"

"Good. Good." He sifted through the papers on his clipboard. "I went through your numbers last night. You're a machine. You blew your goals away this month."

"What were the numbers?" Tom heaved his body out of the pool and joined Sean, looking over his shoulder at the chart. When he saw how much he'd improved his time and distance, he pumped his fist in the air. "Yes!"

Sean gave him a high five. "When you want something, you get it, don't you?"

Tom grinned. "I guess I do."

"I'll let you get back. See you tomorrow."

Tom dived back into the pool. For months he'd been worried about the swim portion of the race. Didn't think he could handle it. Didn't have the swim skills to excel. But he'd been wrong. He could handle it. He was going to destroy the race.

Gliding through the water, he maintained his form.

When you want something, you get it...

In real life, yes. He worked hard, he focused and he went after his goals. But his love life was another matter. Claire's and Libby's voices clamored in his head. *Spell it out for her.*

What did they know, anyhow?

Did he want Stephanie to stay? Macy?

Yes. One hundred times, yes.

Then why wasn't he going after them? Why was he letting her make the decision?

He'd been doubting himself for years. Maybe it was time to prove his worth. He'd let her leave five years ago. Maybe he had more of a say in this than he realized. Maybe he had to try to break down her walls.

He thrust down the lane. He wanted Stephanie back in his life. For good.

Time to fight for her. Time to own his power. Time to convince her to stay.

"Let's get Daddy this!" Macy raced up the aisle and wrapped her arms around an enormous pink-and-black zebra-striped furry pillow. "He'll love it."

"I think you're the one who would love it." Stephanie plucked the pillow out of Macy's hands and set it back on the shelf. "Think about the things your dad likes. What would make him happy?"

She crinkled her nose and set her finger on her chin. "Hmm… He likes running and jumping. We should get Daddy a trampoline."

Stephanie held back a chuckle. "Again, that sounds more like something you would enjoy."

"Everybody likes jumping, Mama."

"Maybe so, but I'm on a budget. Let's look for something in the less-expensive department."

"Where's that?" Macy turned her head this way and that. "Is it by the toys?"

She laughed. Only her daughter would take her comment literally. "Come on. We'll go to the kitchen aisle."

Her conversation with Bea still lingered in her mind. All the way to Macy's day care and back home she couldn't stop thinking about Tom. And the future.

And the more she thought about it, the less she liked the way she held him at a distance. He'd forgiven her. Might even be offering her a second chance. The chance of a lifetime.

When had she gotten so scared?

"What about this? Isn't this the thingy you make shakes with?" Macy pointed to a blender.

"It's a blender." Stephanie picked up the box and examined it. "Doesn't he have one already?"

Macy shook her head.

"This might work. He could make fruit smoothies."

"Or chocolate shakes!" Macy hopped, clapping her hands, her eyes bright. "Oh, I did it again. I want the shakes. Daddy doesn't."

Stephanie ruffled Macy's hair. "Actually, you

picked a good gift. I think he'll like it, and it's okay if you do, too."

"You can have one, too, Mommy. Daddy will make you one if you ask."

She hefted the blender under one arm and held Macy's hand with the other. Tom would make her a shake if she asked. In fact, he'd been extremely accommodating with Macy, with her schedule and even with her grad school choices. He'd given his opinion, but he'd compromised.

He treated her like an equal. Respected her.

And maybe she deserved his respect. She'd carved out a decent life for herself and Macy with the Lord's help and with Dad's. But something was missing, and it wasn't the beach. It wasn't her degree. It wasn't even her close relationship with her father.

Tom held the key to her locked-up heart, and if he offered it to her to be near Macy, maybe in time he could learn to offer it for more.

"Can we get some candy, Mommy?" Macy bent to study the rows of candy bars at the check-out lane.

"Not today." Tomorrow, after the housewarming party, she was having a heart-to-heart with Tom. A blender was nice and all, but he really wanted his daughter.

She bit her lip. This idea forming in her mind turned her stomach queasy. It meant taking a chance. It could mean waiting for him to come around, maybe months or years. She would have no plan B. She'd had too many plan Bs in life anyway.

And this time, the uncertainty didn't terrify her.

She owed it to him, to Macy and to herself to be brave. To lay her heart on the table. And to accept what he decided. Her fate would be in his hands.

Lord, help me.

It would mean breaking Dad's heart. After all he'd done for her. But she'd been supporting herself and Macy for more than a year. She had the strength to do it on her own.

But hopefully she wouldn't have to.

Chapter Seventeen

"Ah, here's our little sweetheart! Come and give me a big old hug." Aunt Sally kissed Macy's forehead. Tom said a silent prayer, thanking the good Lord for his sweet aunt. Sally bent to Macy's level. "Let's get that coat off so you can have a cookie. And don't tell anyone, but I've got a soda hiding in the fridge for you. Oh, and look, there's Papa."

Tom's palms grew moist as Stephanie followed Macy into the foyer. She slipped out of her jacket.

"Here—let me." He grasped it, his fingers brushing hers in the process. Slow heat warmed his core. If he could snap his fingers and make all the housewarming guests disappear, he would.

"Oh, we got something for you." She bent and picked up a wrapped box, then, with a shy smile, handed it to him. "If you already have one, you can take it back. I included the receipt."

"I don't want to return it." His voice sounded dry, and he got lost in her gaze. "Thanks for coming."

She lowered her lashes and nodded. Man, she was pretty. Pretty? More like glowing. Breathtaking. A loud laugh drifted from the living room, where Dad and Uncle Joe talked with a few other guests. Didn't mean he couldn't get Stephanie alone, though.

"Hey." He glanced around. "Do you have a minute? I need to talk to you."

"Sure."

The door opened, and Claire and Reed spilled inside. "Happy housewarming, big brother!" She threw her arms around him and squeezed tight. "Tell this one—" she pointed to Reed "—how awful it is to live in a subdivision. Living on the lake is the best option."

Reed rolled his eyes. "We could walk to the lake if we lived here. This is the premier subdivision in Lake Endwell. Don't you want to pick out kitchen cabinets and carpets?"

Claire grimaced. "Yuck. I hate that sort of thing. If—and that's a very big if—we ever build a home, which we aren't, you'd have to be in charge of it all." She pretended to shiver, then noticed Stephanie off to the side. "Oh, hi, Stephanie! Come here and give me a hug."

Stephanie's eyes widened, but she accepted

the embrace. Tom stepped forward to whisk her away, but Libby and Jake came in.

"I think we need to take this to the living room. Come on." Claire gestured for Stephanie to follow. Tom greeted his other sister. More family and friends arrived, including his employees and several customers. He gave them all the grand tour and an hour later stood in the center of a boisterous group in the living room. But his eyes kept seeking out Stephanie.

There, on the couch next to Libby. The hair on his arms rose. Would Libby say something to hurt her? He inched toward them, but Stephanie leaned back and laughed. Libby angled in toward her, touching her arm. He exhaled.

Time to get Stephanie alone. Before he lost confidence and let his plan fall apart. He couldn't take much more socializing, anyhow, not when his future hung in the balance.

"You must be charging us too much for our cars." Chuck Leeman, one of his best customers, slapped him on the back. "Hello, Buckingham Palace, right?" He nudged Tom in the ribs.

Tom grinned. "I always give you my best price."

"I'm sure you do. Come over here, I've got a couple buddies looking to get into new trucks…"

Tom glanced at the couch, but Stephanie wasn't there. He scanned the open room, saw Macy but no Stephanie. His arms fell to his sides, but he painted on a grin and humored Chuck.

Twenty minutes passed and he finally broke away. A tap on his shoulder had him turning. "When you get a chance—not now, I know you're busy and I don't want to take you away from the party—could we talk? Privately?" Stephanie's eyes darted back and forth.

"Yes. Now." He claimed her hand and led her to the hall.

"Wait, Tom, the party—"

"The party can go on without us." He kept a tight hold and led her up the curving staircase through the upstairs hallway to his master suite. He shut the door and locked it. Then he faced her, wanting to lift her up and trail kisses down her neck. Which wasn't smart, since he had no idea how she would react to what he had to say.

"Are you sure about this?" The question didn't surprise him.

He nodded. Where to start? He'd rehearsed this moment half the night, and now his mind went blank.

Love.

Supposed to spell it out for her. Tell her what she meant to him. Convince her to stay. His mouth went drier than caked mud midsummer.

"I talked to Dad last night." She stood straight,

like a strong sapling in the forest. "I'm not moving to Florida."

"Western accepted you?" There, his tongue loosened.

"I don't know yet, but it doesn't matter. I'm staying here. I'm staying because it's best for Macy."

The hope rising in his soul paused. "Is that the only reason?"

She shook her head, tilting it slightly. "It's not. It's not even the main reason. The last couple of months have been hard—great, but hard on me. You see, I've needed to be in control most of my life, probably because I had so little control when I was young. My parents' divorce threw my world upside down."

He wanted to take her in his arms, but she wasn't finished.

"It made me insecure. When we got married, I didn't trust you'd be there for me. My mom never was. And then you weren't. So I justified spending time with Aaron. Then I saw what a lousy substitute he was, and I was so ashamed. Since then my life has revolved around being someone I could be proud of, and I am. But you came back into my life and all the memories came back. All the shame."

"Don't, Steph," he said, touching her cheek.

"I need to." Her eyes implored him, and he

nodded. "I'm staying here because I love you. I've always loved you. I've never gotten over you. But I'm not trying to trap you into anything. I can wait, Tom. I can wait forever if necessary, but I won't be with you unless it's me you want. Not Macy's mom. Me." She pointed to her chest.

He widened his stance. "What if you don't get accepted into grad school here?"

She shrugged, lifting her chin high. "Doesn't matter. I'll reapply next year. This is what I want."

Taking her hands in his, he processed everything she said. "No, it's not. It's what I want. You want to be a CPA. You want the beach and to see your dad."

"I'll still get my career. I can visit Dad. When I called him last night, he wasn't happy about it, but he's supporting my decision."

"I can't let you do this." He dropped her hands. "You're the one making all the sacrifices."

She couldn't move, but bits of her heart were chipping off with each word he spoke. The pulse in his neck throbbed. Her finger itched to touch it, to soothe the muscles in his arms, bulging with tension. She hadn't meant to get him all worked up. Not at his party. Not like this.

"I guess that's your answer, then." Her words came out clipped, quiet. She'd better get downstairs, say her goodbyes and leave. "Just forget what I said about love and all that. I don't want it to be awkward between us. But I'm still staying in Michigan. I made up my mind."

He blocked her path. "No. That's not my answer. And I'm not forgetting what you said. Why would I ever willingly forget you love me? Why would I throw that away as if it meant nothing? It means everything."

She swallowed. He sounded mad. Or passionate.

"You had your say. Now it's time for me to have mine." He led her to one of two chairs by the fireplace opposite his bed. Kneeling, he rested his hands on the armrests, trapping her. She tried to look away, but he captured her gaze with his.

"What are you doing?" So close she could smell his skin. Clean. Tempting. Too compelling. Whatever he was about to say, she doubted she could argue it.

"I'm fighting for you. Spelling it out."

Her mouth formed an O. Spelling what out? And did he say he was fighting *for* her? Could it be true?

"I love you," he said. "I've loved you since I saw you in that cute collegiate T-shirt at the tailgating party where we met. You were kind. Sweet. Gentle. And I was a stupid idiot for not cherishing you when we were married. I'm not saying I'm glad we got divorced, but maybe we both needed these years to get our acts together. I didn't appreciate you, and after you left, I shuffled through each day. I was living, but I wouldn't call it a life."

His gaze branded her, sending a shiver through her body. "The other night, I was scared. It ate at me. But I'm telling you now, I want to be enough for you. I want to be the guy who is there for you. Who treats you right. Who listens to what you did that day, who holds your hand when you're sad, who celebrates with you when you're happy. The one who eats dinner with you every night and makes you coffee every morning. I love you. I never stopped loving you."

She scooted forward, wrapped her arms around his neck and slid off the chair onto her knees to join him. "Really?"

"Really." Then, the planes of his face straining against his skin, he claimed her lips with his own and pulled her closer, so close she could feel her heartbeat stampeding with his. He kissed her slow, caressing the back of her neck.

"You're mine," he said. "You'll always be mine."

She gasped. "Guess I'm really not moving to Florida."

"Tell me about it." He kissed her again. When she broke away, she nibbled on her lower lip. She still had a few questions. Important ones.

Confusion rippled across his face. "What's wrong?" He let her hair slip through his fingers, and she wanted to bask in his touch, his tenderness.

But she gave her head a small shake.

"Tell me, Steph. You can tell me anything. Remember? We said we'd be honest with each other. I can handle it."

He probably could handle it. But could she?

Stephanie sat back on her heels, all the joy blossoming like a spring flower over her heart, but she had to know for certain. Couldn't have even a sliver of a doubt.

"When we were married," Stephanie said, "I felt unimportant, like you woke up one day and thought you'd made a mistake picking me as your wife."

"I know that now." He nodded as he held her gaze. "I wanted to be successful, to buy a house, start a family. I blew it. After we split, I blamed you for going behind my back, but I hadn't been the man you needed. I wasn't enough for you. But I want to be the man I should have been then. I don't ever want you to question your importance in my life."

His words filled the crevices of doubt, but one crack remained. One she had to be certain of.

"You were always enough for me. You will always be enough. But I have to ask you one more thing." Stephanie touched his cheek with the back of her hand. "Do you love me for me? Or do you love me for being Macy's mom?"

He frowned as he considered. Then he cupped her chin with his hands. "I love you. Stephanie. And I love you, Macy's mom. I can't separate the two, so don't ask me to. I love you. Your spirit. Your morals. But I love you with Macy. You're an amazing mother. You've done it all for years—I have no idea how. So, yeah, I love you for you, but I love you for Macy, too. I'm sorry if that's not what you wanted to hear."

Tears pressed against her eyes. "You think all that?" Her heart filled, overflowed.

"Yes." He nodded, brushing his thumb under her eye as a tear fell.

"I… I think you're an incredible dad. You're so good with her. So patient. I wish I had half your patience. And you play with her—I feel bad for not being as much fun as you are."

"Well, it's easy to be fun. I'm not the one grinding away at school and work and worrying about bills the way you are. I want us to be a family, Steph. I want to take some of the pressure off you. I want to be an everyday dad to Macy."

"I want that, too, Tom. I would love to give Macy a family—trust me, I would. But I think we should take it slow. We rushed into everything last time. Let's spend time together—not only as a family—but just you and me. Figure out what we want, how to move forward."

He yanked her to him. "I agree. And let's start with some catching up." A wicked grin spread across his face. His nose almost touched hers.

"I thought that's what we were doing."

"I'm just following your suggestion." His gaze fell to her lips again. "Getting to know you. Slowly." He kissed her. And she sank into his embrace. Enjoyed his version of catching up.

"Um, shouldn't we get back to the party?" She nodded toward the door.

"Nah. They're fine without us." He turned on the gas fireplace and lowered his body to the floor, pulling her to sit in front of him. Flames rippled upward. She leaned her back against his chest and reveled in the strength of his arms circling her.

"Are you sure about staying in Michigan?" he asked, nuzzling her cheek. "I want you to be happy."

"I want nothing more than to stay right here."

His breath heated her neck. "So by taking things slow, do you think a month would be long enough for that? I've got this big empty house, and it's pretty lonely."

She laughed. "A month is not taking things slow. I have a lot of things I want, you know."

"Like what?"

"Like more kids."

His lips tickled her ear. "I'm on board with that."

A knock on the door made them both twist to see who it was. "Tommy? You in there? A couple of people are getting ready to leave."

"Be right out." He met her eyes, and she giggled.

"I don't remember the last time I felt this naughty." She rose to her feet.

"You're about to feel naughtier." He tugged her back down and kissed her again.

She kissed him back. "Okay, okay. We have to get back to the party."

"Why?"

"Well." She thought a moment. "I can't think of a single reason."

"That's why I love you."

Epilogue

Stephanie arranged the corn husks around the pillars of the porch. She'd draped a plaid wool throw over the rocking chair she purchased last weekend. The perfect spot to read to Macy. Three pumpkins waited to be carved. Claire and Reed had promised to stop by later to help. Overflowing pots of maroon mums flanked the door, and a crimson mat welcomed guests. Home. Her home with Tom and Macy. She raised her face to the cloudless bright sky and smiled.

"Hey, gorgeous." Tom ambled behind her, wrapped his hands around her waist and pressed his cheek to hers. "Looks good. You sure know how to make this house a home."

She twisted to kiss him. "I've been thinking about having a house for many years."

"Good thing I snatched you up, then."

Stephanie straightened the husks. "I thought I snatched you up."

"Well, you couldn't help yourself. It was my awesome finish at the IRONMAN that won you over, wasn't it?"

She laughed. "Considering we got married a week after the race, I'd say no. But I am proud of you. Under twelve hours. Just like you wanted."

He brushed her hair from her face and stared into her eyes. "Eleven hours and forty-two minutes. Get it right, Mrs. Sheffield."

She swatted his shoulder. "You're going to be impossible to live with now, aren't you? What time are you aiming for next year?"

"Time? I'm aiming for…a baby. Girl. Boy. Doesn't matter."

She couldn't stop the grin spreading over her face if she wanted to. "Really? Are you sure you're ready?"

"I'm ready. And I'm aiming for eleven hours for the race. I want it all. Starting with a kiss." He pressed his lips to hers, and she wriggled her arms around his shoulders.

"I like the way you think."

"Daddy, Daddy, look at me!" Macy wheeled down the driveway on her purple bike with pink sparkly streamers. "No training wheels!"

Tom pressed his forehead to Stephanie's. "Duty calls."

"Well, you are the Iron Man after all."

He winked, jogging toward Macy. "Don't forget it. You realize you're going to be the envy of all the ladies."

She laughed. "I already am."

"And I'm a blessed man."

* * * * *

Dear Reader,

Thank you for spending time in Lake Endwell! The Sheffield siblings have so much going for them—faith in the Lord, love for each other, a lucrative family business and a charming community. Nothing in life is perfect, though. Even people who seem to have it all struggle. Tom Sheffield lacks the thing he wants most, a family. And Stephanie paid dearly for the poor choices she made, but through her faith in God, she gained the courage to tell Tom about their daughter. God used their little girl to bless them with a family.

I can relate to Tom because I think we all sense something missing in our lives from time to time. And Stephanie isn't the only one who's made poor choices; I have, too. When we focus on God's will instead of our own, we gain peace in our hearts regardless of our circumstances. There is no sin or problem too big for God. He hears you. He knows what you're going through. Depend on Him!

I love connecting with readers. Please stop by my website, www.jillkemerer.com, and email me at jill@jillkemerer.com.

God bless you!
Jill Kemerer

LARGER-PRINT BOOKS!

GET 2 FREE
LARGER-PRINT NOVELS
PLUS 2 FREE
MYSTERY GIFTS

Love Inspired®

Larger-print novels are now available...

LARGER-PRINT BOOKS!

GET 2 FREE
LARGER-PRINT NOVELS
PLUS 2 FREE
MYSTERY GIFTS

Love Inspired®
SUSPENSE
RIVETING INSPIRATIONAL ROMANCE

Larger-print novels are now available...